ARCHITECT

Don Lohnes

ISBN

Hardcover: 978-1-967668-81-6

Paperback: 978-1-967668-80-9

Architect – *one whose profession is to design and draw up the plans for buildings, etc., and supervise their construction.*

Architecture – *The science, art, or profession of designing and constructing buildings or other structures.*

Funk & Wagnalls New Standard College Dictionary of the English Language (1913)

Acknowledgements

I could not have written this book without the assistance of John Mogan, a personal friend, whose command of the English language was most helpful in ensuring that what I wrote did not come across like I had just finished a grade school English test. John and I met several years ago over a cup of coffee and continue to do so whenever time permits. He has written several books himself and was also very helpful with my first book "So You Want to Build a House" published in 2014.

Secondly, I would like to thank Andy Lynch, FRAIC, fellow architect, who has been patient with me in reviewing my writings, a few times, and providing corrections and thoughts where needed.

Lastly, I wish to thank Nancy Bateman, a retired Superior Court Judge of Nova Scotia for her assistance in regards to the trial portions of this book. She was most helpful with the timelines and language needed to be, for lack of better words, legally sound.

Dedication

I dedicate this book to architects the world over. Architects create the spaces required for living, working and playing. We, as architects, have the ability to think in the third dimension, which is not how most people think on a day-to-day basis. We have knowledge of building materials, both strengths and weaknesses, and how they fit together to best form the built environment.

However, because the legal profession tends to throw the net wide in legal proceedings, architects sometimes get caught up in legal matters that may not be warranted, which is one reason for this book. I am not saying that we do not have to be accountable for our actions, because we do. Architectural and construction matters may not always be understood by the court system. Various forms of arbitrated solutions by professionals have been found to be more effective.

This book is a work of fiction. Names, characters, and incidents either are products of the author's imagination or are used fictitiously. Any resemblance to persons living or dead is entirely coincidental.

Contents

Preface

Lonnie Donaldson was again working late at the office. It was early fall 2019 and this project was due to go out for bids the following week. The client, Transportation and Infrastructure Renewal Department, (TIRD) wanted to maintain the schedule they had set for the project, a new P – 9 school for Middle Musquodoboit in order to keep the local member of the Nova Scotia Legislative Assembly happy. Coordinating the pre-bid documents was not an exciting job for an architect, but paramount to a successful project.

Occasionally he would look out from his office located on the penthouse level of Metropolitan Place, Dartmouth. The view across the harbor to Halifax was impressive and he enjoyed watching the cruise ships when in season. Two docked at Pier 21 at that moment. He dreamed of a time he and Patricia could take a few cruises someday.

Patricia, Chloe, Ben, and Barbara were probably enjoying a final round of golf at Old Ashburn and then a fine meal on the deck overlooking the eighteenth hole. If he was lucky, there might be some leftovers when he arrived home later in the evening, so he decided not to order out. He would open the bottom drawer of his desk and take out a bottle of Glenlivet Scotch and a Montecristo No.4. Knowing that the air handling system would remove the cigar smoke from the office by morning before the staff arrived, he snipped the end of the cigar and lit it. He enjoyed watching the smoke rise to the ceiling as he exhaled. Then he poured three fingers of scotch and sipped slowly as he watched the lights coming on in the buildings across the water. In the harbor the ferry service was operating as usual, both ferries leaving their respective docks of Halifax and Dartmouth in unison and passing in the middle of the harbor.

Suddenly he heard, "Lonnie, are you smoking those damn cigars again?" It was Betty, one of the office's cleaning staff.

"Oh, hi Betty, the air handling system will take care of it before morning," he replied.

"Yeah, but it still stinks while I am working here," was her retort. Then she said, "I will come back later, got other floors to do before I finish up tonight."

As Betty departed, he glanced back to the drawings, and looking at drawing 704 he noted that the electrical engineer had specified a pot light housing that would extend fourteen inches above the finished ceiling. This conflicted with the structural drawings that had a concrete beam located in the same position. Lonnie made a note to inform the electrical engineer that a revision would be required. He added this to the list of other conflicts and items that need to be dealt with before finalizing the construction documents. The fewer change orders on a project, the better.

Around nine p.m. Lonnie decided that enough was enough and it was time to head home for the night; the rest could wait until the morning. The cigar smoke smell was almost gone by now. Lonnie packed his briefcase, then decided to leave it where it was until morning. Walking toward the front entry to get his coat from the closet, he began thinking that retirement was not that far off. He and Patricia could do without the burden of working every day. But until that day arrived, there were still several projects to be completed and hopefully he could sell the firm to some of the senior shareholders.

He put his coat on and after setting the security alarm behind him, he headed to the elevator. He descended to parking level two and while walking to his car, he thought he heard someone call his name. He turned toward the voice, a voice which sounded all too familiar. Next, he heard "Lonnie, you son of a bitch," then he heard two gunshots. It felt like someone punched him hard in the chest. Lonnie put his right hand to the location of the pain; it felt wet and he had a nauseated feeling. Then a third shot rang out. As he lay on the cold concrete, he thought he heard sirens in the distance. He struggled to maintain consciousness.

CHAPTER 1

The Second World War had just ended in 1945 and things were starting to settle down around the globe. D-Day in Halifax, Nova Scotia was quite a celebration, known as the Halifax VE-Day riots of May seventh and eighth. What began as a celebration of the end of World War II victory in Europe rapidly declined into a rampage by several thousand service-men, merchant seamen, and civilians who looted the Cities of Halifax and Dartmouth across the harbor. Tensions had been building for over six years as war transformed Halifax from a small and conservative maritime city into what a British admiral called the "most important port in the world," as the Canadian Headquarters of the Battle of the Atlantic and the western terminus for the vital North Atlantic convoys to England. By 1945, Halifax had become a bustling, overcrowded, underserviced port city.

There were huge lineups to get into the city's few restaurants. Lohnes' Restaurant on Blower Street was one of the two more popular places to dine for a good home cooked meal; the other was the Green Lantern. At Lohnes' you could get a good meal for forty-five cents, but you were asked to leave when finished because others were waiting to eat. There were no legal places to get a drink, but there were dozens of illegal ones. Locals complained that the military purchased most of the stock on the shelves during this time leaving nothing for them to buy. Due to the large number of military personnel in town, organizers decided on VE-Day to shut down the tram service, to discourage sailors from going downtown. Liquor commission outlets, restaurants, retailers and movie theaters all decided to shut and shutter their premises, ostensibly to prevent trouble.

Rear Admiral Leonard W. Murray believed his sailors had won the peace and deserved their chance to celebrate. So late on the afternoon of May seventh, the day Germany surrendered; he overruled the advice of his senior officers and allowed more than nine thousand of his men to go ashore for the night. By midnight downtown Halifax was filled with more than twelve thousand who had no place to eat or relax. Rioting broke out, tram cars were set ablaze, windows were smashed, liquor stores looted, and merchandise stolen. Three people died, 363 arrested, 654 business damaged and 207 establishments looted to some degree. Total price tag of damage and looting was over five million dollars.

A Royal Commission blamed the riots on the failure of the naval command to control the sailors, and particularly on the Admiral. The following year Rear Admiral Leonard W. Murray resigned in protest to the board's findings.

CHAPTER 2

Meanwhile, on the south shore of Nova Scotia, the Charles Donaldson family, oblivious to the goings on in Halifax, resided in a two-story wood frame home, with the typical Lunenburg Bump on the front elevation, a few houses up river from the LaHave River cable ferry landing on the east side. The LaHave ferry had been operating, in this location, since 1918 and consisted of a Cape Island boat with a barge-type ferry attached by rope to the boat, with a capacity of six cars. It departed on the half hour from each side of the river. You could set your watch to the ferry schedule.

Sarah Donaldson, Charles' wife, and daughter Margie enjoyed their location on the river. Margie was almost two years of age, having been born in July 1944. Sunsets were wonderful and the salt air was most pleasing. The Donaldson property consisted of a home, a barn, a garden, and a few acres of pasture with the balance of the thirty-five acres as woodland. The timber, when cut sporadically, provided additional income. Charles would see to it when needed. They also had a cow for milking, a few chickens for fresh eggs, and the garden provided fresh vegetables in late summer and early fall.

Charles was fortunate, for at the moment he had a full-time job with the Ritcey and Creaser General Store in Riverport, just a couple of miles down the river. Elijah Ritcey was very good to his staff if they were good at what they did and were also dependable. Charles was both. The store was located on the main street in Riverport and backed onto the LaHave River. It was located close to the Ritcey Brothers

Fishery, one of the largest fish-producing plants in Nova Scotia, at its Kraut Point facility in Riverport.

Because of a leg injury from falling out of a tree in his youth, Charles was not accepted to fight for his country during the Second World War, although he did try to enlist. Perhaps this was a blessing in disguise. He was kept up to date on the progress of the war by the *Progress Enterprise* which was published daily in Lunenburg and sold at the Ritcey and Creaser Store.

Charles enjoyed his work and his co-workers at the store. They handled just about anything needed for the fishing fleet that used Riverport as its base. It was also the general store for the local area, providing hardware and groceries. One day in February of 1946, Elijah called Charles into his office and said, "Charles I understand Sarah is with child again, and I just wanted you to know that anything you need, please just ask, as I would be happy to help." Charles expressed his thanks to Elijah and left his office. It was comforting to know he had the support of his employer.

At this moment, the dragger *Rose Marie* needed provisions; bait, line and hooks, salt, and ice along with the staples of food for the crew prior to its departure to the Grand Banks. They would be gone for approximately two weeks at a time. Charles knew most of the captains by first name and most of their respective crews. This made the working relationship with each boat much easier for everyone. Heck, come any weekend he might be having a cold Keith's beer with any one of them at the local pub. It took over six hours to get the boat stocked for departure the next morning at high tide. His co-workers, Obediah Oxner, Gabriel Zink, Harold Lohnes, Bob Mossman, and Robbie Creaser, had separate tasks for each part of this process. This was a typical day at the store.

In all, there were eighteen boats in the fleet that sailed out of Riverport. Schedules varied depending on weather, supplies, crew, and tides. Sometimes double shifts were required since it was important to keep the fleet well stocked and out on the banks fishing. Charles did not mind the overtime required; the extra dollars were well received and Sarah was very understanding.

CHAPTER 3

Springtime 1946 was fast approaching and there was work to be done at the Donaldson residence along with the day-to-day work at the Ritcey and Creaser Store. The garden had to be tilled in preparation for seeding. The barn needed minor repairs and so did the house. Winter had been typical for the location, some snow and some ice damage, but nothing exceptional. After shifts at the store and available weekends, the required work around the home got completed quickly. There was also time to prepare the second child's room since Margie was almost two years of age and she enjoyed her own room now. The house had additional rooms and the one next to Sarah and Charles's bedroom made an excellent room for the child on the way.

Sarah started into labor on June nineteenth at ten twelve p.m. Charles was prepared with all the necessary items packed and by the door in the front porch. Margie was taken next door to the Whynott's for the rest of the evening since it had been pre-arranged well in advance. Arthur and Carla were more than pleased to help their neighbors. Charles and Sarah got in their 1941 Ford and headed to Dawson Memorial Hospital in Bridgewater. The hospital was built in 1920 and served a considerable area around Bridgewater. Sarah was looking forward to the birth of a new baby and was fully prepared. Charles was driving as fast as he could, given there were no streetlights and the possibility of hitting a deer existed. Plus he had to try and avoid any of the many potholes that existed. They arrived at the hospital twenty-two minutes after leaving home. The staff immediately took over and Charles started to relax.

In the early hours of June 20 Charles and Sarah were blessed with the birth of an eight-pound, seven-ounce boy with ten toes and ten fingers in perfect health. Charles was very happy since he had secretly wanted a son. Sarah was resting peacefully from the labor. Charles enjoyed holding his newborn son. After he placed him in the bassinet under the watchful eye of the duty nurse in the nursery, he looked for a place to lie down for a few hours for a much-needed rest. He found a couch and quickly went into a dead sleep for several hours.

When Charles woke, he looked in on Sarah and his newborn son, and then drove back to East LaHave to check on Margie and to let the Whynott's know the good news. Arthur and Carla were very happy for Charles and Marge and since their son, Michael, was only a few months older, he now would have a playmate next door. Margie was happy to have a baby brother.

Next, Charles drove down to the Ritcey and Creaser Store to let Elijah know of the recent birth. Elijah offered congratulations and said, "Charles, take a few days off until things begin to settle down at home." He added, "Almost all of the fleet is out on the banks now, so it is quiet at the store for the moment." Charles appreciated the kindness expressed by Elijah and the rest of the staff at the store. Charles bought some cigars and gave everyone in the store one.

Charles headed home to fix lunch for Margie. Afterwards they drove back to Bridgewater so that Margie could see her baby brother. Sarah was awake and breastfeeding the new born. He was a hungry lad. All three discussed possible names for him. Consensus was reached with the name of Lonnie, and the name on the birth certificate was Lonnie Ross Donaldson, Ross being Sarah's maiden name. Sarah would be home in a few days, so Charles and Margie left them both resting peacefully and returned home. On the doorstep was a fruit basket and bouquet of flowers with a note of congratulations from his co-workers at the store. Life was good for the Donaldson's.

CHAPTER 4

The next few years passed quickly, and Christmas of 1948 was approaching. Margie was four years of age, and Lonnie over two, and becoming quite a handful. It was mid-December and there was not much snow on the ground yet. Charles and Margie were out looking for a Christmas tree. They had walked up the hill behind the house on their search for the perfect tree to decorate their home. Sarah had moved the furniture around in the living room in preparation for its arrival. Boxes of ornaments were brought down from the attic for the evening decorating.

Lonnie was playing peacefully, thank God, on the floor with his building blocks, building skyscrapers or the like. He seemed to enjoy building anything and he was almost in a trance when he was doing things like that. He was walking at this stage in his development, and when not building things, he would try to get into cupboards to play with the pots and pans.

Sarah was busy doing her Christmas baking: fruitcakes, shortbread cookies, and of course the family favorite, chocolate chip cookies. Those were hard to keep in the cookie jar. Charles and Sarah had decided which of the turkeys in the yard would be sacrificed for Christmas dinner. Charles would take care of that when the time was right for proper butchering and hanging before preparation for the oven. The Whynott's were coming for Christmas dinner this year so there would be nine for the evening meal. The Donaldson's would be spending Christmas Eve with the Whynott's for the annual consumption of fish chowder. The chowder consisted of a few potatoes, carrots, onions, haddock, shrimp, scallops, and lobster cooked in water with a heavy cream added before serving, and a final touch, it was sprinkled with bacon pieces. This was a becoming a tradition because the families alternated the location each year. The kids got along great and were becoming the best of friends.

Charles and Margie went in search of and found the perfect tree and Charles cut it down. He hoisted it on his shoulder and they headed back down the hill to the house. Margie was full of cheer and happy to spend time one-on-one with her father. As dusk fell, you would see the lights coming on in the houses across the river in the community of Pentz. Charles could tell that their friends the Sullivan's and the Daugherty's were home because he could see the lights from both their houses and their outside Christmas lights were very colorful. He took the time to point out their houses to Margie. She enjoyed the time she was able to spend alone with her father because he was usually very busy at work both at the store and when he was home.

Back at the house Sarah had put a fire on in the fireplace and the wisps of smoke rose towards the sky. The pleasant smell of a wood fire was in the air. Charles and Margie both were looking forward to enjoying the warmth of the fire when they returned with the tree. When they arrived back home with their prize, Sarah had the tree stand and the lights and ornaments ready for decorating the tree. Charles placed the tree in the stand and made sure it was secure before he would allow anyone to start. The first ornament to be placed on the tree was the Christmas Angel, which Charles looked after, and it went to the very top of the tree. Charles was careful to be sure that the electrical cord was hidden at the back side of the tree. Next, he placed the lights around it. Margie was picking out the ornaments, carefully since they were very delicate and could break very easily. Margie, Charles, and Sarah all participated in the tree decoration. Lonnie peeked in once in a while and participated by adding a few ornaments, but he was too busy building something with his building blocks.

After all the ornaments and decorations were hung on the tree, the garlands placed, and the lights turned on, they all stood back to admire their work. Even Lonnie stopped what he was doing to come and see the tree all decorated. Charles and Sarah poured themselves eggnog fortified with a little brandy, a Christmas tradition they continued since they had their first Christmas together. Next Sarah returned to the kitchen to finish preparation of the evening meal. All were called to the table, with Lonnie in his highchair. Supper that evening was pan fried haddock, potatoes, carrots, and peas with fresh melted butter. Charles got the haddock off one of the boats that docked for supplies that morning. The carrots and potatoes were from the garden harvested early that fall and kept in barrels of sand in the basement cold room. The peas were canned.

Christmas morning arrived and Margie and Lonnie were both excited about the gifts under the tree. They noticed that Santa had taken a few bites from the chocolate chip cookies and he finished his glass of milk that they had left for him. Charles and Sarah enjoyed watching their children open their gifts and their excitement. Breakfast became brunch and both children played with their new toys for the rest of the day until it was time to get ready for Christmas dinner with the Whynott's.

The Donaldson family got dressed for dinner and waded through the new fallen snow to the house next door. Once the winter clothes were off both Lonnie and Michael disappeared as Michael wanted to show Lonnie his new Lincoln Log set. That kept them both busy until it was time for dinner.

Charles supplied the turkey this year and the Whynott's prepared the rest of the Christmas meal. These family meals were a joint effort. Everyone enjoyed the turkey and the dressing. The dressing was made from potatoes, carrots, onion, butter, bread crumbs, sometimes sausage and summer savory, lots of summer savory. Carrots, mashed potatoes, yellow beans, and peas rounded out the meal. Desert was a special fruitcake made by Carla. While the parents enjoyed the fruitcake the kids had vanilla ice cream with chocolate syrup.

CHAPTER 5

Lonnie and Michael became the best of friends. Seldom would you see one without the other; they were like two peas in a pod. The summer of 1952 they both were six years old and that was the year when Michael got a bike for his birthday. Early in June, Michael was trying to describe what it was like to ride a bike to Lonnie. He described a feeling of freedom, almost like a bird, floating along the roads without a care in the world. He never mentioned the scrapes he received from his falls when he first learned to ride his bike.

After some verbal instructions, Michael got Lonnie to sit on the bike and gave him a push towards Riverport on the road. As Lonnie was coasting and peddling away, he heard Michael say, "Back pedal to stop," but at that moment a car came around the corner and Lonnie headed for the ditch, which thankfully was covered with grass so the landing was soft and the bike was not damaged. After a few laughs, scrapes, and scratches Michael explained how to stop the bike and Lonnie climbed on again, eager to learn how to ride. The second attempt was successful and soon Lonnie was riding like a pro. The bond between Michael and Lonnie was growing stronger. They were the best of friends.

That night at supper Lonnie could not stop talking about bike riding. How much he enjoyed it. While he never asked his parents for a bike they could tell that he wanted one. He was also quite proud of the scrape on his knee that occurred when he fell off the bike and onto the dirt road.

Charles and Sarah thought it over and bought a bike for Lonnie's birthday that summer from the Ritcey and Creaser store. With an employee discount, it did not set them back too much. Lonnie and Michael peddled all around their homes and all the way to Riverport. They would go swimming in the "bare hole" when the tide was in. The bare hole was beyond Riverport, close to the fish plant. There was a two-by-ten board stuck under the bridge for jumping off. The water was always warm since it was shallow and heated by the sun. Everyone in the community knew these two by their first names and everyone kept an eye out for them. This was comforting for Sarah and Charles.

They never got into too much trouble when together, except maybe for the grass fire they set one day while playing with matches. Michael had taken a box of matches from his parents' kitchen drawer and was showing Lonnie how they worked. He was lighting them and dropping them on the ground. He got Lonnie to light a few and to drop them also. One of the lit matches landed in an area of dry grass and a small fire started. The boys tried to put it out but it soon got out of control. Shortly afterwards they heard the local fire station bells and a fire truck arrived on the scene. That resulted in bringing the local police to their homes and biking privileges were suspended for a week. Both Charles and Arthur subdued a laugh because they both recalled their youth and the trouble they used to get into, but kept stern faces in front of the boys. Without bike privileges the boys played between the houses and their friendship grew stronger.

Michael's father had a .22 rifle and he showed Michael how to use the rifle in a safe manner. Soon he was hitting bullseyes on a regular basis. Michael's accuracy was unbelievable, easily hitting the O on a can of Campbell's soup at twenty paces. He showed Lonnie how to load the gun and how to aim and both had fun shooting cans or bottles. Michael really enjoyed shooting and became an excellent marksman and Lonnie, while not so good, could at least hit the target close to the bullseye on most occasions. They tried to light matches like they saw on TV, so they drilled holes in a log to stand the matches up in. Occasionally they would break one, but they could never light one. Michael came very close a few times but ended up just knocking the head off the match; his accuracy was scary given his young age. Michael was very comfortable holding and firing a gun, in fact too comfortable.

CHAPTER 6

Lonnie and Michael had started school the previous fall at the Oceanview School in Rose Bay. This school was not large, but it handled all the kids from the surrounding areas of Kingsburg, Upper Kingsburg, Rose Bay, Lower Rose Bay, Bayport, Lower LaHave, Middle LaHave and Feltzen South. It was a P–12 school and some classes were combined due to the limited number of students. Parents had to arrange to get their children to school and this was usually done by carpooling or walking. Since this was a community school, everyone worked in a positive way to get their children educated. It was the parents' responsibility to make sure their children got to school in a safe manner. It was not that difficult because there were not many problems to consider at that time. For most of the school year, except for snow days, Lonnie and Michael rode their bikes to the school. The roads were not busy so they could ride down the middle of the road unless a car or cars were present. They also had to avoid those students that were walking to school. Locks were not needed because nobody in the community would think of stealing bikes, especially from kids. The roads, while not paved, were graded twice a year by the Department of Highways.

Another of the highlights of the summer months was the long pedal over to Hirtle Beech and a visit to Gladys Canteen for lemon meringue pie after a quick swim in the cool Atlantic waters off the beach. They were in their early teens and girls became an interest to both of them. Hormones were flowing. The boys grew into fine young men and were well known in the community.

That fall they both were in grade nine, the year was 1960.

Not students that excelled in their grades, they did pass their exams and were both average students. They played on the school basketball team and although the school could not field a football team, they did practice the sport during the regular gym classes when weather permitted. They did not have a sports field on school property, so football practice was limited.

The school years passed quickly. Sometimes Charles would take Lonnie with him on his trips to Lunenburg for supplies he needed for the farm. When Lonnie was fourteen, during the month of July, Charles had to go into Lunenburg to get fertilizer for the garden. He took Lonnie with him and before they returned home they stopped at the Lunenburg dairy. While they were there, Lonnie met Angus Walters who was sitting on milk can drinking chocolate milk. Lonnie had heard his name before, but he could not recall why he had heard of it. On the way home Charles explained that Angus Walters was the captain of the Bluenose, a sailing schooner that was famous for winning five international sailing races. Charles reached in his pocket and took out some change and showed Lonnie the image of the Bluenose on the Canadian dime. Lonnie did a little more research in the library on Angus Walters when he got to school the next day. Lonnie was inspired by this small man that had achieved greatness because of his sailing skills.

CHAPTER 7

Arthur Whynott was a cabinet maker by trade. He turned out some very fine furniture from his workshop on his property. Most of his work was sold by word-of-mouth and some pieces was carried by Elijah at the Ritcey and Creaser store. He worked mostly with birch and oak, but sometimes walnut if he could get a hold of some. His shop was fully equipped with a table saw, band saw, drill press, lathe, sander, thickness planner, edge planer, and a number of hand tools including various clamps. His work was widely recognized and sought after around the South shore.

Sometimes when Michael was not around to play with Lonnie, Lonnie would sit in the workshop and watch Arthur work his magic with the tools and the wood. He was fascinated with what could be constructed from what was at one time a tree. One day Lonnie questioned Mr. Whynott, "Can you show me what each tool does for you?" Arthur talked to Charles later that evening and asked if it would be all right to teach Lonnie about the use of power tools and Charles was not only pleased that Lonnie wanted to learn, but happy that Arthur was willing to teach him. Soon, when time permitted, Lonnie was operating most of the tools under Arthur's careful supervision and turning out some nice pieces.

Michael was not interested in what his father did for a living nor the time he spent with Lonnie. Michael was not going to spend his time working in a workshop; in his mind he had more important things to do with his life. First and foremost his dream was to get away from Riverport and live in a big city.

Lonnie secretly made Christmas presents for his dad, mom, and Margie for the following season. Charles was getting a boot jack made from birch, Sarah a knife block made from oak, and Margie a jewelry box made from birch. For the jewelry box he had to get some hardware from the Ritchie and Creaser store without Charles and his family finding out. Some hinges and a clasp for the jewelry box. So one day, after discussing with Arthur what was needed he peddled to the store, when his father was not there, and described what he needed to Elijah. Elijah knew all the employees' children; they were a close knit community. Elijah helped Lonnie pick out what he thought was required for the jewelry box and discussed this with him. Lonnie said that the first hinges he was shown were too large for the box he was making, so Elijah picked out some other ones and Lonnie was sure that they would work just fine. Elijah enjoyed the close relationship he had with his workers and their families. Lonnie put the items in his knapsack and peddled back to Arthur's workshop to get them installed. Elijah spoke to the rest of the staff working that day and mentioned that they were not to mention to Charles that Lonnie was in the store that day.

Each piece of wood was carefully sanded and then finished with high gloss polyurethane for protection. Lonnie was very proud of his works and Arthur was very proud of his pupil. Next Lonnie searched for boxes so he could wrap each of his gifts. He did the wrapping in his bedroom and hid the gifts under the bed until Christmas Eve. He waited until everyone was asleep and then he went downstairs and placed them under the tree. He was proud of his accomplishments and had a great feeling of satisfaction of working with his hands.

CHAPTER 8

As Christmas approached in 1960, Lonnie and Charles went in search of the perfect tree. Sarah had prepared the living room and had retrieved all the ornaments for the family to decorate the tree. Lonnie found it that year and he cut it down with the buck saw he had with him. His father helped carry it back to the house. This year it was the Donaldson's' turn to host the annual seafood chowder on Christmas Eve and then they would go to the Whynott's for turkey dinner on Christmas Day. These family traditions together were enjoyed by everyone.

While the typical opening of presents was overwhelming for all, the gifts that Lonnie had made for his family were very well received by each and every one. Margie was very happy with her jewelry box, now she had a place to keep her prized possessions, and she got up and went over to Lonnie and gave him a hug and a kiss on the cheek.

Sarah was happy to get a knife block instead of keeping the knives in a drawer; now they were easily accessible on the kitchen counter. She immediately went out to the kitchen and took all the knives out of the drawer and placed them in the knife block. All knives fitted perfectly; Lonnie had pre-measured each one before he started his work on the project.

Charles would no longer have to struggle getting his work boots off and so the boot jack was kept in the back porch. Lonnie had difficulty hiding his pleasure at his family enjoying his creations. At dinner that evening Charles thanked Arthur for his kindness and time he spent in his shop with Lonnie.

Arthur said that Lonnie had an interest in making things and was very creative in working with his hands. He was more than welcome in the shop at any time.

That year the Donaldson's were celebrating their twentieth wedding anniversary, having been married late December in 1940. They had made plans to go out to a New Year's party at Elijah Ritcey's home in Riverport. Margie and Lonnie were all too happy to spend the evening with the Whynott's. All had plans for an evening of fun to ring in the New Year. The Ritcey and Creaser store had another successful year and to show his appreciation, Elijah invited all the staff and their spouses to spend New Year's Eve at the Ritcey's' home. This was a large home, yellow gold in color with the main view due north up the LaHave River. The guests enjoyed an excellent meal of prime rib roast, cooked to perfection, oven roasted potatoes, carrots, parsnips and onions, Yorkshire pudding, and horseradish, with either apple pie with a slice of cheddar cheese or blueberry pie and vanilla ice cream. Following the meal, the guests relaxed in front of the fire in the parlor. At midnight the New Year was rung in with much laughter and merriment by those in attendance.

At one point the men collected in one area of the house and the ladies in another and all were deep in conversation. Charles was explaining to his fellow workers his hopes for the future of his children. He secretly hoped both his children would continue their education and meet a partner in the future to share their life and raise a family. He was looking forward to having grandchildren.

Sarah was discussing with the ladies the family plans for a summer vacation for a few weeks at their cousin's cottage in

Merigomish, Pictou County. She knew the children would enjoy trips to Melmerby Beach. The children were at an age now that this would most likely be the last summer they would all spend together as a family as the children's thoughts for the future were formulating. Also there may be some shopping in Halifax on the way to and from the cottage.

At 12:52 am the Donaldson's decided it was time to head home after a very enjoyable evening. They were driving a 1956 Pontiac station wagon, a vehicle which allowed for the family to drive in comfort on trips around the area. They were going by Indian Path road and Sarah was discussing how the station wagon would be great for their upcoming summer vacation when a pickup truck came out of nowhere, ran through the stop sign, and struck them broadside, killing Sarah instantly. Charles was badly injured and just barely alive. However when the station wagon hit the water due to the impact from the accident, he soon drowned, as he was pinned between the seat and the steering wheel.

The local police chief was called immediately by the first officer that arrived on the scene after the accident had occurred. Part of the necessary and unpleasant duties of being the chief of police was to inform the family of the victims. And so the police chief arrived at the Whynott residence early in the morning of January first to inform them of the accident. Lonnie and Margie were devastated. They asked Carla and Arthur to call their uncle and aunt in Halifax, Robert and Mary Ross.

Robert and Mary drove down to the Riverport area the next morning, arriving before noon, and took the children back to the Donaldson home. Funeral arrangements were made very quickly with Robert taking the lead. Both Margie and Lonnie were not much help, as could be expected. Mary spent most of her time comforting both of them.

The joint funeral for Charles and Sarah was held on Tuesday, January third in Bethany United Church, Rose Bay, and attended by most of the communities around the Riverport area. The church was at capacity and the adjacent hall was set up for the overflow of local citizens wishing to pay their respects. Margie and Lonnie were both in shock; their world had been turned upside down in an instant. The Whynott and Ross families were there for support and looked after both children during that time of turmoil. Burial was in the church cemetery.

The reception was held in the church hall after the service was completed. The locals brought sandwiches of all different kinds with the crusts cut off. There were also sweets and coffee and tea available. Robert and Mary were with Margie and Lonnie at the receiving line. The children thanked those that had attended; they both were still in shock.

These deaths caused grief up and down the shores of the LaHave River. Both Margie and Lonnie overheard at the reception that the driver of the pickup truck, who was very intoxicated at the time of the accident, was arrested when he was released from Dawson Memorial Hospital and charged with vehicle homicide.

Robert was mentioned in the will of Charles and Sarah not only to be the guardian of both Margie and Lonnie, but also the executor of the will. The children were the sole recipients of the house, land, and any funds left in the joint bank account.

Robert was pleased that Charles and Sarah had taken his advice and prepared a will, since that saved considerable time and problems in dealing with the family possessions.

Robert said to Arthur and Carla, "It would be best for Margie and Lonnie to move to Halifax with he and Mary since they were the closest family members and they had no children of their own." He went on to say, "The house will be put up for sale and each of the children will inherit fifty percent of the family estate, in accordance with the family will." Everything was sold within a few months and Robert invested the money for Margie and Lonnie. The funds would be available when they turned twenty-one. Since Margie was in grade twelve and Lonnie in grade ten, new school arrangements would be required.

CHAPTER 9

Robert and Mary lived at 1978 Beech Street, across from Sir Charles Tupper Elementary School in Halifax. It was a central location, close to just about everything. The Candy Bowl was on the corner of Quinpool Road and Beech Street, and the Oxford Theatre was only a block away on the corner of Quinpool Road and Oxford Street. The Ardmore Grill was on the corner of Quinpool Road and Elm Street. Both Margie and Lonnie were out of their normal element and not sure what they would do. Robert and Mary were in the same situation because they were not used to children. Mary had been unable to bear children, although she had always wanted to. Now she was an instant mother of two teenagers and not sure what to expect. Both of the children were withdrawn and of course saddened by the loss of their parents.

For their first evening in Halifax, Robert and Mary took them to the Ardmore Grill for supper and then to a movie at the Oxford Theatre. While both had been in Lunenburg to a restaurant with their parents previously this was the first time that they had been to a restaurant in Halifax and a movie theater. The movie playing at that time was *Ben Hur* starring Charlton Heston. Both Margie and Lonnie were totally engrossed in the movie and couldn't stop talking about it afterwards. It helped to ease their grief. On the way back to the house they stopped at the Candy Bowel and Robert picked up some chocolate bars, jujubes and mints. Before retiring that evening both Robert and Mary mentioned to them both that if they needed to talk or had any questions that they were available at any time.

After the children had gone to their respective rooms, Robert and Mary talked about the situation that they were now in. Neither had ever thought that they would have children; however, you don't plan for these situations, and you just have to deal with them. And they both were prepared to do whatever was necessary to make their instant family work for everyone.

Both Margie and Lonnie were fortunate to have their own rooms and a place to study in peaceful solitude. Robert had them both enrolled in Queen Elizabeth High School after a few days in Halifax. This was the Protestant school, and the Roman Catholic school, St. Patrick's High, was just across Quinpool Road near the Willow Tree intersection. The staff from the school were most accommodating given the circumstances of their plight and tried to help Margie and Lonnie in any way they could. The principal, Len Hannon, was very helpful and understanding. Margie was in her last year of high school and not sure what the next year would hold for her. Lonnie was in grade ten and there were sixteen grade ten classes in this school. Both were quite shy because this school had over sixteen hundred students between grades ten and twelve. The school they came from had only eighty six students from primary to grade twelve. There was a huge change for both of them.

For the most part the kids at the school were friendly and outgoing and tried to engage both of them first in conversation and then in school sports. Time heals many things and soon both Margie and Lonnie were coming out of their shells and getting more relaxed with their new environment. They could not forget the tragedy that had taken away their parents, but they had to move forward.

While Margie was thinking of what she would be doing the following year, Lonnie was thinking of trying out for the football team. Some of his new friends convinced him to try out during the spring training sessions. Robert thought it would be good for Lonnie to get involved with sports, but also wanted him to think about working during the summer to earn some money for college, should that be of interest to him. Robert had a friend in the construction business; he was building some new homes in the Fairview area, not far from Beech Street, and the bus system could be used for travel back and forth to work. Lonnie was receptive to this idea. The job was secured and when school finished that spring. Lonnie went to work for Redding Construction.

Meanwhile, Margie, with Mary's help, got a job at the Royal Bank on the corner of Quinpool and Oxford Streets, becoming a teller. She became very interested in the banking process and enjoyed the interaction with the bank's customers. After July had passed, she decided to enroll in the secretarial program at Maritime Secretarial School on Bell Road. Both Mary and Robert thought this was an excellent choice and quietly applauded her decision. She was accepted in the program and classes began in September. It was a two-year program to achieve certification.

CHAPTER 10

Lonnie started his summer work period by meeting Garth Redding, the owner of Redding Construction Limited, and then was introduced to the surveyor. The surveyor showed Lonnie the subdivision survey plan, which located the soon to be constructed streets and the housing lots. Next the surveyor gave Lonnie a quick tour of the property describing what was necessary to begin its development and then he pointed out on the survey plan where the survey makers were located and then showed Lonnie the actual corner pins of the property to be developed. As they walked from corner marker to corner marker the surveyor pointed out on the survey plan where they were. Soon the layout started to make sense to Lonnie.

The surveyor began the process of laying out the soon-to-be streets, which were surveyed and the area cleared of trees. The streets were rough graded by bulldozers and trenches excavated for sewer and water services. Sometimes rock, when encountered, had to be blasted with dynamite to be removed. All the workers would stand under the upside-down bucket of a Payloader, for protection against flying rocks, when the blast was made.

After the streets were prepared for pavement the lots were surveyed and survey markers were placed on all the corners of the lots so the future landowners would know the extent of their property. Lonnie worked alongside the surveyor and his helper, Ralph Millwood. Ralph was a bit of a character, but enjoyable to work with, although you never knew what kind of mischief he might get into next. Things like bumping the tripod with the transit so that the surveyor had to reset it again and again. Lonnie had no choice but to let the surveyor know what was going on so that there were no errors in the survey. Ralph got an earful that day but just laughed it off.

Next the building lots were surveyed and corner pins were placed so that owners would know the full extent of their property. Each owner would receive a certified copy of their house lot for their files.

Then the area for the foundation was excavated, and the footings for the foundation walls were placed. The house foundation formwork was constructed from tongue and groove boards, whalers, and spacers, and held together with bailing wire. Next the walls were braced in readiness for the concrete pour. The spacers were removed as the level of cement rose within the formwork. The tough part of that job was wheeling a wheelbarrow full of fresh and heavy cement on the narrow wooden ramps. After the cement had set up for a few days, the formwork was stripped and the nails removed so that the boards could be used for sub-flooring, exterior walls boards, and roof decking. The finished foundation walls, once they had set up, were then called concrete.

Window and door openings were carefully measured in each of the exterior wall framing sections. Called "rough openings" they were always approximately one inch larger or more than the windows and doors that would eventually be installed. The rough opening space allowed for the windows and doors to be leveled and set in place with shims, and without concern about whether they would fit in the openings. The remaining rough opening space between the window or door frames would be insulated prior to the installation of wallboard and trim.

One day Lonnie and Ike Smith were sheathing-in a roof with four-by-eight sheets of plywood. When the last sheet was to be placed a strong wind blew through the window and door rough openings and caught the sheet of plywood they were carrying, and almost took both of them off the roof. Fortunately, both he and Ike were quick enough to let go of the plywood and cling to the roof. They logged that memory away for future reference.

Lonnie opened an account with the Royal Bank, close to home and where Margie was employed. There he deposited most of his fifty-dollar per week earnings, keeping some for his own enjoyment, perhaps a quick stop at the Candy Bowl on his way home, and the purchase of the necessary work clothes and boots. Payday was always on Friday with cash in an envelope. The work was an excellent experience in the field of construction.

As September approached and the school year opened, Lonnie left his work and began his studies in grade eleven. He had over six hundred dollars saved in the bank. Prior to leaving his summer job, Mr. Redding asked, "Lonnie, did you enjoy your summer working construction with us, and will you consider returning to work next summer?" Lonnie replied, "Yes, I enjoyed the work and I was hoping you would ask me, I will be back for sure, thanks."

CHAPTER 11

On his travels back and forth to work on the bus, Lonnie noticed a sign for the Ashburn Golf and Country Club off Dutch Village Road. One evening he asked his uncle what it was all about.

"It's a place where the game of golf is played," said his uncle.

Lonnie said, "That game sounds interesting, could we try it sometime?"

Robert responded, "Sure, I will investigate what is involved and then we can check it out." Robert thought that it would be a good way for the two of them to strengthen the bond that was developing between them. True to his word, Robert investigated and found that membership that year would cost one hundred and fifty dollars in dues plus an entrance fee of one hundred dollars for him. For Lonnie, the junior membership fee was one hundred dollars plus an entrance fee of seventy-five dollars. Robert joined them both in 1961 for the total sum of four hundred and twenty-five dollars.

They both took lessons from the Ashburn professional Frank Fowler, and both developed a love for the game. They would usually play nine holes after work. Lonnie, rather than taking the bus home, would walk to Ashburn from work and Robert would meet him there. On weekends they would sometimes play thirty-six holes. Soon they were entering competitions and while they did not win much they both met many other members all from different walks of life. When they were not playing they were watching golf on the television. Arnold Palmer was their favorite player at that time.

One day when Lonnie arrived after work Frank Fowler said, "Lonnie, you seem very interested in golf; perhaps if you came in early one morning, before work, I could help you with your game."

Lonnie asked, "Does tomorrow morning work for you?"

The next morning Lonnie took the six a.m. bus on Quinpool Road to Ashburn and he and Frank teed off about six-thirty. Frank explained a few things about the length of backswing and follow through, and that hitting the ball hard was not required. He said, "An even tempo swing will produce better results than trying to hit the ball hard."

After several attempts Lonnie started to get the hang of it and was hitting nice shots with a slight draw at the end. After about an hour, they had played five holes and then headed back to the clubhouse on hole eighteen. Lonnie expressed his thanks and left for work, but not before Frank suggested that they do this a few more times. For the rest of that summer Lonnie met with Frank in the early morning, on Wednesdays, and Lonnie's game improved greatly. They worked on drives, iron shots, chipping, and putting. Lonnie thanked Frank for his kindness and free lessons.

CHAPTER 12

Physically, Lonnie enjoyed the additional strength he gained over that summer from the labor-intensive work he was doing. Football practice started a week before classes. Since Queen Elizabeth High School did not have a football field, practice took place on the Halifax Commons. Coach Bob Douglas worked with all of the students who tried out for the team. Some were eventually cut, but Lonnie survived. His position was second string, tight end, number seventy-two. Practices were held after classes two to three times a week depending on whether there was a game that week. The archrival was St. Pat's High School. Mary and Robert tried to attend the games in support of Lonnie, and Margie did when she did not have classes. Lonnie was not a football hero; he did not get played the same amount like the rest of the team, but when he did play he played his position fairly well. The relationships that Lonnie developed amongst the teammates were excellent.

When football finished in the fall, basketball started. Lonnie tried out for the team and his assigned position was a forward. He would usually score about ten to twelve points a game, not a lot but certainly acceptable. He met other schoolmates through basketball season and some from other schools that they played: St. Pat's, Halifax West, and Dartmouth High. He was beginning to feel a bit better after the tragedy of the previous New Year.

The YMCA on South Street had several programs for youth. Lonnie attended Twix Teen dances on Friday nights to the sound of all the latest hits coming mainly from south of the Canadian border, and Hi-Y programs where he joined the Epsilon club. The goal of the Hi-Y program was to create, maintain, and extend to the fullest capacity of one's ability, through the home, school, and community, high standards of moral character through improvement, brother/sisterhood, equality, and service in high schools.

Again, Lonnie met some new people in his classes and some became friends for life. There were three guys in particular, and it seemed they were always seen together. While they all went to QEH they actually met at the YMCA with the Hi-Y club. They really connected and were later known as the Big Four. They would always meet after school and walk home together as each one lived off Quinpool Road.

These guys were about as close to family as one could get without being the slightest bit related. Robert and Mary enjoyed each one of them and soon they were visiting their house on Beech Street like it was their second home. Mary baked chocolate chip cookies on occasion but they never seemed to last with these guys around. Lots of times on Saturday at noon time they would all meet for hamburgers and a Coke at the Ardmore Grill before they set off on their adventures for the day. Each of these boys took pride in showing Lonnie around the city. They showed him the various bus routes and soon he was able to go almost anywhere using public transit. Soon the passing of his parents was becoming a distant memory, not forgotten, but it was time to move on with his life. Bob, Skip, Ken, and Lonnie cemented a friendship that would last for many years.

Each of these guys did canoeing in the spring and they invited Lonnie to join them for a canoe trip during the long weekend in May. Robert let Lonnie use his camping gear. The boys had two canoes and Skip's older brother drove them to the Nine Mile River just outside the city where they put the canoes in. from there they canoed down river and ended up in Shad Bay. Robert was able to pick them up with his friend's truck. They had a great trip and lots to talk about.

Robert also gave both Margie and Lonnie driving lessons. They both were soon eligible to apply for their driver's licenses, but both were nervous due to the death of their parents in a vehicle. However, both had to move on and they advanced very quickly and Margie took the required Department of Highways exam that summer. She passed the exam without any difficulty. Lonnie had to wait until the following summer after his sixteenth birthday, and he also passed the test without any issues. Both Margie and Lonnie had realized that driving was not the issue in regards to their parent's accident; it was an accident and accidents unfortunately happen. Occasionally Robert would let each one use the family vehicle.

CHAPTER 13

During the winter of 1962, Epsilon Hi Y Club organized a ski trip to Wentworth Valley, about ninety miles from Halifax. An Acadian Lines bus was rented for the day and thirty-six students took the one and a half hour trip to Wentworth. Bob, Skip, Ken, and Lonnie were on that trip and not sure what to expect, as it was the first time skiing for all of them. They all rented skis, boots, and poles at the ski hill and soon fell in love with the sport.

During this trip Lonnie took notice of a particular girl, and found out from other classmates that her name was Patricia Burton, an attractive young lady. She had dark hair tied in a ponytail, smooth complexion, and an attractive figure. He had also noticed her at school a few times previously, but this time, something about her stood out and he became very interested in getting to know her better. During the morning he noticed her in the line for the chair lift several times. After lunch he saw her skiing down the Rosebowl trail and noticed that she was a fairly accomplished skier.

Lonnie asked Bob, Skip, or Ken if they knew her. Neither of them did but mentioned that they had seen her at Twix Teen dances and that she never seemed to be with one particular male person, so perhaps no boyfriend. That was a good thing.

He watched her on the ski lift a few times and skied down the same trails she did. Once, later that afternoon, when she fell while on the Beaver trail he went over to her to see if she was okay and helped her back up on her feet and to get her skis back on. She was laughing at herself all covered in snow but quickly brushed it off. He introduced himself and she told him her name, and they ended up skiing a few runs together before the time came to get back on the bus for home.

On the way back from Wentworth, on the bus, he made sure he sat across the aisle from her and they continued their conversation from the ski hill. The trip home passed very quickly since they talked about school, families, his loss of his parents, and the fun they had that day skiing. They also talked about their plans for the future after high school. Lonnie made a point and asked for her phone number, and if she would mind him calling her. She blushed and replied, "443-3471," which he wrote down on his arm with a ballpoint pen.

Several other trips to Wentworth were organized that winter and Lonnie and Patricia took part in all of them. Lonnie noticed that the ski hill used felt markers to change the number of ski days on the lift pass. He made sure that he had a few different felt pen colors each time they went skiing. The thirty-third day of skiing was easily changed to a thirty-eighth day with the same color pen and a free day of skiing was the result. Not something that was talked about with other skiers in the group.

They both enjoyed skiing and soon were seen together on a regular basis: on the slopes, at school, and at the Twix Teen dances on Friday nights at the YMCA. Patricia lived with her parents and younger brother in the Westmount subdivision on Robert Murphy Drive. Since Patricia did not stop talking about Lonnie that spring, Lonnie was invited to dinner with the Burtons, Roger and Gail and brother Jasper. Patricia's parents wanted to meet this guy that she kept talking about. Not to be outdone, Robert and Mary invited Patricia and her parents and brother to a bar-b-que before school finished that June. Robert and Mary wanted to meet Patricia and both Patricia's parents for that matter. They all clicked and soon both families were spending time socializing together. They enjoyed each other's company and Robert and Roger found out they had a lot in common.

CHAPTER 14

Lonnie went back to work for Redding Construction for the summer of 1963 and Patricia got a job at Digby Pines Resort waiting on tables in the main dining room. Occasionally they would talk on the phone, but long-distance calls were expensive, so they wrote postcards to each other every few weeks.

Postcard to Lonnie, July 7, 1963

Dear Lonnie,

Life at the Pines is interesting, but it is certainly not like the city. Digby is just a small town. It is well known for scallop fishing and I have to admit they are very tasty. I have met a local girl named Pearl Williams and she has shown me around all the hot spots, not that there are many, but enough that if you were not careful you could get into trouble. Pearl would say, "Not trouble, just good times." She is such a scamp and we are enjoying our times together.

Miss you, Patricia

Postcard to Patricia, July 21, 1963

Dear Patricia,

Construction work is moving forward at a good pace. I am really enjoying working with my hands and in this field. This could be my future. Most of the single family homes are completed now and the developer is looking forward to the next phase of construction. Can't believe that I am looking forward to getting back to school, but then we can be together again.

Miss you also, Lonnie

Postcard to Lonnie, July 30, 1963

Dear Lonnie

Pearl has shown me all around the area of Digby. She has her driver's license and has borrowed her father's car a few times and we drove down the shore to as far as Meteghan and shopped at a second hand store called Frenchie's. That was fun. I bought a nice fall coat for five dollars. See you soon, miss you a lot.

Patricia

Postcard to Patricia, August 12, 1963

Dear Patricia

Summer will soon be over and I am actually looking forward to getting back to school because you and I can be together again. I am enjoying my time in construction and next summer we will be constructing apartment buildings. Football practice starts soon and I am looking forward to that this fall. Also looking forward to some swimming with the boys at Kearney Lake before the water gets too cold. See you in a few weeks.

I miss you a lot.

Lonnie

During that summer Pearl had invited Patricia to the family home in Bear River for the occasional meal. She enjoyed both her mom and dad. Patricia kept in touch with Pearl when she went back to school that fall.

August was coming to an end. Both Lonnie and Patricia's work for the summer was finishing and they began preparing for their last year of high school. Patricia returned home from Digby a week before school started. Lonnie met her at the train station, gave her a big hug and a passionate kiss. They both discussed all the things that had happened during the summer at great length. They missed the close connection they had developed and it was becoming stronger. Lonnie had borrowed Robert's car and he drove Patricia home to Robert Murphy Drive and spent some time with her and her family before returning to Beech Street.

CHAPTER 15

Both Lonnie and Patricia returned to QEH that fall in grade twelve, their final year. Their first date after school started was a breakfast at the Ardmore Grill on the second Saturday in September. While there they discussed what they wanted to do after high school. They also discussed what the future may hold for them as a couple. They both knew that the other was a major part of their current and they hoped their future life; the question was would that continue as they sought to continue their education. Time would tell.

Lonnie was sure that some part of the construction industry held his future and had begun looking into the engineering and architectural professions. Frank Milne, one of his teachers, was very helpful in providing some guidance for his continuing education. They had several discussions regarding his construction experience and how much he enjoyed that field and how that may fit into his coming years. Architecture seemed to be his best path for he always enjoyed creating and thinking in the third dimension and that was something that came naturally. Frank suggested a few books for Lonnie to read about the profession of architecture. One such book was "The Fountainhead" by Ayn Rand. After he and Frank finished their conversation Lonnie went to the school library and signed out a copy.

Patricia expressed an interest in nursing for an occupation. The sight of blood did not phase her in the least and most importantly she enjoyed helping people. She had investigated thoroughly what the requirements and courses were to become a nurse and then registered in the nursing program at the

Victoria General Hospital. Her parents thought that this was a good choice for her and they also thought that Lonnie was heading in the direction that would include a successful future for him.

For the moment, football was on Lonnie's schedule, along with basketball and many visits to the Burtons. His football coach, Bob Douglas required that each member of the team have a complete physical by a doctor. He didn't want any team member to have health issues that could be life threating while on the football field. Lonnie passed all these tests with flying colors.

He and Robert still played a fair amount of golf whenever they could during the week after school and on weekends and soon he had Patricia interested in the game. One fine Saturday in early October Lonnie took Patricia with him to Ashburn. She walked with Lonnie as he played and questioned him about the game. They talked about the various aspects of the game and the simple fact that it involved over four hours of walking and enjoying the outdoors. She could not get over how green the grass was and the texture of the grass on the greens and it was then that she expressed an interest in learning more about the game.

Lonnie did not want to teach Patricia the wrong things so he arranged a few lessons with Frank and she really enjoyed them plus she was a very good student. The following spring she also joined Ashburn, to learn more about golf, play with Lonnie, and also some of her school friends who were members. Frank kept a watchful eye on Lonnie's golf game for he saw potential in the lad. School reduced his time on the course along with football, basketball, studies and, of course, Patricia took most of his only other available time.

CHAPTER 16

This year passed very quickly and springtime of June of 1964 was very busy for both of them and all the other graduating students. There was studying for final exams, the debutant ball and graduation. The final exams were during the second week in June and the debutant ball was held during the third weekend in June on Saturday evening at the Lord Nelson Hotel, on Spring Garden Road. The girls all wore evening gowns and the boys looked good in their tuxedos. Lonnie rented his tux from Dugger's menswear and looked pretty smart but Patricia stole the show in the gown she selected. They were a smart looking couple and both enjoyed the dinner and dancing that evening. After the dance was over Robert was there to drive them both home, first Patricia and then Lonnie.

Graduation followed the next week. Patricia was valedictorian for the girls and delivered a very excellent recollection of her time in high school. She took that time to not only thank her teachers but to also thank the many students that made her time at Queen Elizabeth High School a very memorable occasion, and one that she would not forget. It was appreciated by all students and teaching staff and earned her much praise for her public speaking talents. Lonnie was very proud of Patricia. He was just happy to graduate since he did have some difficulties, but most were overcome by hard work and the help he received from his teachers.

Patricia was accepted into the Dalhousie School of Nursing and started working at the Victoria General Hospital shortly after high school graduation. Not only did this provide some income for her university tuition but the experience gained was second-to-none.

Lonnie went back to work for Mr. Redding that summer after graduation. Since the subdivision he had started working in was nearing completion, he had experienced almost all of the process of building single family homes, from the ground up. Mr. Redding had an area in the subdivision zoned for multiple housing so that summer he had begun the construction of two multiple unit buildings. Each building contained eight apartment units and Lonnie found this kind of construction more challenging than single family homes. The necessary fire protection between units, secondary exits in the event of emergency, and sound considerations between units were all new things to consider.

Lonnie researched where he could attend university prior to entering the School of Architecture because two years of pre-engineering were necessary requirements to enter the program. After some deliberation, he chose Saint Mary's University because the class sizes were considerably smaller than those of Dalhousie. He could have gone to Acadia or Saint Frances Xavier University, but those would have required living in residence and being away from Patricia. In addition, the costs would have been higher, and so he did not look any further for a suitable university.

That summer he purchased his first car using his construction earnings. It was a green 1952 Riley 1.5, which cost him fifty dollars. He and Patricia would take drives outside the city when time would permit. A favorite spot was Crystal Crescent Beech, just past Sambro. Walks along the beach or shoreline, holding hands and the occasional kiss were all part of the time they shared together along with family meals at both homes.

Sometimes when he was not with Patricia, his high school friends Bob, Ken, and Skip would go out to Kearney Lake for a swim; the water was nice and warm during the spring and you could dive off the rocks along the shoreline. Bob was the real swimmer; his dives from the highest rock were like a knife cutting the water. Lonnie was not prepared to test fate with a high dive. The rest of them just enjoyed swimming in the warm lake waters.

This was the last summer they would spend together as those three were all going to Ryerson University in Toronto. Bob was registered for journalism, Ken hotel management, and Skip electronic equipment repairs. They tried to convince Lonnie to join them but his mind was made up, architecture was his passion. Lonnie would miss his school friends, but had to get on with his own education; finally he knew the direction that he was heading in and that did not involve going to Toronto. Lonnie also knew that no matter where these guys ended up they would always remain in contact with each other as their friendship meant a lot to each one of them.

Lonnie had asked Robert and Mary if they all could come back to the house on Beech Street for a bar-b-que in August before the other three departed for Toronto. They had no issues and Robert made his special hamburgers and Mary prepared a summer salad, some cookies, and had some soft drinks for the boys. Bob was the cookie monster, he would sometimes stop by for a cookie when in the neighborhood even when Lonnie was not home. Mary gave them all hugs before they left.

After his friends had departed for Toronto, Lonnie was thinking of what he wanted to do that September. He was not sure that he wanted to go to school then. He also discussed this with Patricia and she said for him to follow his heart and he would find the right path.

CHAPTER 17

After much deliberation, and several discussions with Robert, Lonnie decided not to go to university that fall. Instead, he went back to work full time with Redding Construction. He enjoyed the work, the physical activity, and being outside for most of the day. What he was really interested in was that Redding Construction had just won the contract for a ten-story office building in Dartmouth on the waterfront. While this would involve additional costs to travel the bridge each day, he knew that the experience would be worth it. And he also got a substantial raise. Patricia was not sure of his decision, but she understood it was best to let him do his thing.

After the site was excavated for the foundation, a large concrete pad was poured just outside the extremities of the building. That was the base for the soon-to-be-installed tower crane. This would be the first time that he had worked on a site with one. The first section of the tower crane mast was bolted to this concrete pad. Next a mobile crane began hoisting each section of the crane mast to the previous section until it reached the point where the boom was added. The boom is much like a weather vane, since it had to be able to move freely with the wind. The operators cab was located on the boom next to the mast. This process went very quickly and was completed in two days.

The main structure and each floor of the building were of reinforced concrete. Lonnie learned how to read the structural drawings and to see where the reinforcing steel was required to be placed. Not only that but he spent some time working with the crew tying the rebar to other pieces of rebar. For each of the floors and columns concrete pumper trucks were used to get the concrete to the correct location. He moved up with the firm and soon was put in charge when the foreman had to leave the site.

That year passed quickly and Lonnie had gained considerable experience in the construction industry. Mr. Redding wanted him to stay with the firm, but Lonnie replied in the negative; he was now more determined than ever to go to the school of architecture. He wanted to learn and be involved with the design and construction of buildings since he now had a very good introduction to how some were constructed.

He bid farewell to Mr. Redding and thanked him for his kindness and all the things that he had learned. Lonnie did ask if he could return the next summer to work with the company. He received a very positive, "Yes, of course, we would love to have you back with us for another summer."

CHAPTER 18

Tuition for the first year, 1965, at Saint Mary's University was five hundred and eighty dollars, and Robert helped with a portion of the cost for the books. Again, Lonnie met many new classmates, a few like Bill Martin and Dave Penny became good friends since they also played golf at Ashburn. Other classmates were only acquaintances during their times at school. The pre-engineering class had twenty-six students and they all worked side by side each day so they got to know each other during class time, but not to the point that they socialized on a regular basis.

Courses included English, chemistry, engineering, physics, philosophy, surveying and, physiology. Lonnie was the only one headed for architecture; the rest of the students, like Dave Penny, were going into various branches of the engineering profession. Dave was going into Industrial Engineering. Since the campus was relatively small compared to Dalhousie University, Lonnie met many other students pursuing different fields of study. Bill Martin's plan was to study medicine, became a radiologist, and hopefully end up working at Dartmouth General Hospital, near where grew up.

Lonnie went back to Redding Construction the following summer and picked up where he left off the previous year. The office building in Dartmouth was nearing completion. The aluminum skin and glass curtain wall panels were being installed along with the interior partitions. Most of the building was already rented to various professional firms. One of note was the law firm of Broady Clarkson. That firm had special requests for the finishes in their offices. Things like hard tile in the lobby, granite countertops in the lunch and board rooms, and solid core doors for all the offices. Lonnie met Tom Broady during this finishing period and he was impressed with his demeanor.

Lonnie's co-workers questioned him about university; some teased him about being a college boy and others were impressed with his determination to become an architect. During lunch breaks a few questioned him on the requirements, so he briefly described that it required two years of pre-engineering and then four years at the school of architecture to earn a Bachelor of Architecture degree. Then after graduation, depending on where he could find employment, it took a minimum of two years of working with an architect to qualify for membership in the Nova Scotia Architect's Association (NSAA). Most of the co-workers thought that it took too much time but applauded his determination. Following this work period he went back to complete his second year at St. Mary's.

During that the fall of 1966, the new library opened on St. Mary's campus. The university was growing. Lonnie and Bill Martin were both on the Saint Mary's golf team that fall. The university tournament was held at the Brightwood Golf Course in Dartmouth, Bill's home course. While the team did not fare well in the overall team competition, Lonnie himself had a personal best: his first hole-in-one, which was on the seventeenth hole. One hundred and fifty eight yards and he used an eight iron.

The SMU Huskies were the undefeated football champions that year. Time passed quickly. Sometimes it passed too quickly. The second year went fast, although uneventful, and soon Lonnie was preparing to go to Nova Scotia Technical College (NSTC) to complete his desire for a degree in architecture.

He went back to work with Redding Construction the following summer on a new library for Dalhousie University. Again he gained more knowledge in the construction field. This building was using waffle floor slabs. They looked similar to an upside down egg carton, but what this type of construction allowed was up to forty feet of span so it decreased the number of columns. He became very familiar with the placing of the pre-fabricated concrete forms for the floor slabs and soon was taking a lead role in the preparation of each of the floor slabs being poured. He did not forget to mention to his co-workers about his hole-in-one during the university golf tournament.

That summer passed very quickly and he and Patricia spent as much time together as time would permit. She was very busy with nursing and he with construction. All too soon he was preparing for his time at the Nova Scotia Technical University School of Architecture.

CHAPTER 19

The School of Architecture was located in the former Nova Scotia Museum building on Spring Garden Road. Tuition was not excessive and the income that he had banked certainly helped with the cost and the books needed for that year's studies. He had set up a drafting table in his room on Beech Street where he could do some quiet work away from other students. He soon found out that the professors liked to see the students in the studio, so he planned to be in the studio during their usual visit times. When at home, if an idea came into his head in the middle of the night he would get up and sketch it out before it escaped him.

Since Lonnie was still living with his aunt and uncle, costs were relatively low, aside from operating his car. Other students, especially those that came from outside the province, had to live in residence or find an apartment or some other form of accommodation. Student residence spaces were limited.

The school hours were not regulated. Students could work in the design studio 24/7 if that was their wish. The professors would pass in and out at all times just to see if students were working on their projects or if they needed guidance. If you thought you were finished early, they might point out something that you should reconsider. And of course you would, because if the professor saw that you paid attention to his suggestions, your mark might be higher.

All-nighters were common with projects due at nine a.m. the next day. Group projects were sometimes the work of just a few of the group. The others seemed to find other things to do and relied on their teammates to help them get through the work. Lonnie found that all-nighters not very productive for him because trying to resolve a design problem when sleep deprived resulted in bad decisions on his part. However, sometimes they were un-avoidable. For those nights, Lonnie would try and get some sleep late in the afternoon in preparation for the long night ahead.

He found his best hours for thinking were early in the day and he would sometimes arrive around five a.m., after picking up a coffee at a local coffee shop, before others joined him in the studio. This was his best time of the day for design problems. Not only was he more productive, but the pen or pencil seemed to flow much better at that time.

Sketching classes were led by one of Halifax's well-known artists. Some classes were held in the school, some were outside, and sometimes road trips were involved, Peggy's Cove being one of the more popular spots. He tried several types of mediums: pencil, charcoal, and fingers. The goal was to take your thoughts, and then bring them to life on a piece of paper based on what you were looking at. That was intriguing.

Drafting was undertaken on a drafting board with a parallel bar, triangles, and a pencil. Students that could afford them purchased drafting machines, but they still had to be operated manually. An eraser, required to remove errors, sometimes resulted in messy drawings, but that was the way it was. Only the brave would draft with pen and ink.

CHAPTER 20

Lonnie played flag football against the other students in the engineering faculty. Each of the engineering departments fielded teams for various sporting events. The friendships were good for the campus and many followed after graduation. Some of the engineers Lonnie wanted to work with after graduation so he made sure he had their contact information for the future. The architecture students had a good team with a former quarterback from Acadia University. They defeated each of the engineering teams throughout the first year.

The architectural school also hosted dances in the design studio, depending on the workload at the time. Student desks were moved to the side to provide room for dancing. It was a great time to relax and not think about school. Patricia joined him for these dances when she had a break from nursing. That gave Lonnie an opportunity to show her around the school of architecture and perhaps to steal a kiss when no one was around. Lonnie mentioned that the dance was being held in the design studio and then took her downstairs to the lecture theater, H19 was the room number. He also showed her the photo studio, the carpentry shop, and several of the regular classrooms in the building. Their relationship grew and remained strong.

There was one good thing about the school of architecture: it was close to the Piccadilly Tavern on Grafton Street and Lohnes Restaurant on Blowers Street. Both places served good food when a break was needed from studies and home cooking. Of course at the Pic, the known nickname for the tavern, Alexander Keith's pale ale, a local ale, was an all-time favorite.

One day at lunch over a few beers, Lonnie told a story about Alexander Keith.

"Apparently Alexander was leaving his office one evening on Hollis Street and just as he exited the building he met one of the Ladies of the Night. Since Alexander at that time was running for mayor, he was trying to win all the votes he could so he said, 'Och now how's business?' She replied, 'Business is so good that if I had a second pair of legs I would open in Dartmouth.'" That story got several laughs, even from adjoining tables.

Again, Lonnie went back to work for Redding Construction the following summer and this time they were constructing a small shopping center in Bedford. The job site was close to home and he would sometimes stop and play a few holes of golf on his way back to Beech Street. Ashburn had a new pro now since Frank had retired. His name was Jay Lohnes and he was a former classmate of Lonnie's from Oceanview School in Riverport. He and Lonnie remembered each other and sometimes when time permitted, Jay would join Lonnie for a few holes. Patricia was now working full-time at the Halifax Infirmary since she had graduated from nursing school in the spring of 1969.

Lonnie's construction experience was very evident during the classes on construction techniques. He got along very well with his construction professor, Valid Lyman. Professor Lyman was pleased that someone in the class had some construction experience, and he relied on Lonnie several times during classes. It was a good asset for the profession.

As time passed, Lonnie eventually needed his own space and after second year, moved in with some of his classmates to an apartment on Cherry Street. It was not a party house; they all had various projects to work on to complete their studies. Some set up studios in their respective bedrooms and would spend hours designing and redesigning their projects. Of course, laundry and cooking meals became part of the everyday process. Lonnie also worked part time at a local ski shop, not far from the apartment, to earn extra cash for rent and food. Each of his roommates took turns cooking the evening meal and of course they all tried to outdo the next guy. When time was tight, due to studio time at the school, fish sticks and rice became a simple staple.

Laundry was done on Saturday morning. Lonnie would go to the laundromat on Quinpool Road and put his clothes in the washing machine and then go for groceries at Sobeys across the street and by the time he got back the attendant at the laundromat would either have the clothes in the dryer or finished, folded, and ready to go. Lonnie appreciated the friendly service he got at that laundromat.

Some days, depending on the weather, Lonnie would walk to the school: east on Cherry Street, south on Robie Street, east on Julibee Road, south on Summer Street to Spring Garden Road and on to the school. Sometimes he would walk through the Public Gardens for a change. On the Spring Garden Road side of the Public Gardens some local artists—Roger Hupman, Judy Matthews and sometimes Julie Walker—would be there with their artwork for sale, hanging on the fence. Lonnie, since he walked past them often, he got to know each of them very well and would stop and admire their latest pieces of art. They were all College of Art and Design students and income from the fence sales helped pay for school, meals, and lodging.

CHAPTER 21

Lonnie's professor at the school of architecture, Valid Lyman, was helpful in getting him a job with Wilson, Harris and West or more commonly known as WHW, for that summer. They were a local architectural firm located in the Bayers Road Shopping Center. Professor Lyman made sure that he mentioned Lonnie's construction experience and that he had considerable knowledge of construction techniques. That was well-received by the firm. He was hired as a draftsman and worked on several projects under the watchful eye of the chief draftsman, Harry MacKenzie. Harry was very competent and helped Lonnie learn the proper way to write specifications and where to look for the correct information in doing so. The firm had an extensive library of construction material catalogues which were updated on a regular basis by the product salesmen or saleswomen.

The development of Clayton Park off the Bedford Highway was just beginning and Lonnie was tasked with the design of one of the new homes on Bayview Rd and he also worked on a curling rink project in Chester, Nova Scotia. He enjoyed both projects and Harry helped with a few details but Lonnie's experience while working with Redding Construction was very evident. The fact that he could translate what was drawn on paper to reality was an asset.

WHW were impressed with Lonnie's construction experience and took him out on some larger projects to further his experience. On one occasion he noted and pointed out a detail that was bound to leak after a few years. He explained to

Harry that the flashing was not properly installed and showed him how eventually water would find its way into the building. Harry made note of this deficiency and reported it to the general contractor so that correction could be made in a timely manner. Harry was embarrassed that he missed it. Since it was properly detailed on the contract documents it was the contractor's responsibility to correct the deficiency and no additional cost to the contract was incurred.

Lonnie considered this experience extremely valuable and informative for his next two years of school. His experience in construction and classes with Valid Lyman were instrumental in the knowledge he retained.

CHAPTER 22

In the meantime, Michael had previously graduated from high school at Oceanview, and also worked part-time at the Ritchie and Creaser store. He was not interested in university, so after finishing school, he searched for work in the area. Work was scarce, and he had little or no training in a specific trade, but he was a good talker and could sell things to almost anyone. Eventually, he got a job selling architectural products like carpets, vinyl flooring, hardwood flooring, and ceramic tile. His territory started with the south shore of Nova Scotia and then eventually encompassed the western part of the province. Sales were good and Michael did very well financially. He was soon driving a fairly new car, a 1966 Chevrolet convertible. It was a chick magnet and he had no trouble finding girls to date. But he never seemed to be able to settle down with one specific person. His sales job had him traveling a considerable amount and a few times, while in Halifax for a sales meeting, but not always, he would look Lonnie up and they would go for something to eat, usually at the Ardmore Grill for a hamburger, fries, and a cherry Coke.

Lonnie enjoyed connecting with his old friend but as time went on he noticed that things were different, quite different from their times on the LaHave River. He couldn't put his finger on it, but there was a difference and he was concerned for his old friend. Michael was boasting about how successful he was in sales and how easy it was to make money.

Michael became well-known in the sales industry and was well respected. Soon he was off to Toronto as he had landed a job with a national firm that sold roofing materials and products. His territory increased to also service the Maritimes and he was on the road eighty percent of his time. He enjoyed the travel, expense account, and other perks that came with the job and, of course, the money. He was spending it as fast as he was making it and not saving for down the road.

National companies would observe how sales were going and if sales in a particular area seemed to exist on its own—that is, the salesman had out done his or her work—then they might be moved to another division or they might be let go. So even with Michael's excellent sales ability, sometimes, he would find himself out of a job. He did learn to bounce back by looking for products that were not selling well in Eastern Canada and he would approach those specific companies and convince them to hire him to sell their products. He almost always had work and developed a good reputation in the sales industry.

Lonnie was becoming very concerned about his old friend; he was familiar with the body, but the mind was not the same.

CHAPTER 23

The third year in the school of architecture was uneventful, the design work and the dialogue with the professors continued on a positive note. Lonnie was finding the workload a little more manageable now as he was getting accustomed to how the school operated. He had developed a good relationship with the professors and they found his construction experience invaluable for his future in the profession. He still managed to do the required all-nighters, but made sure he had a nap late in the afternoon so he could hopefully stay on top of things during the wee hours of the morning.

Finally the fourth and last year of school came around. During that year architectural students were introduced to computer-aided drafting, better known as CAD. The initial version of CAD was a machine about eight feet square and six feet high. This machine was introduced to the students in their last year of architecture. To have this CAD machine draw a room with a door and a window, you had to punch holes in FORTRAN cards, as they were called, and then feed them into the machine. Then the machine would print out the room plan like you had drawn it. Heaven forbid if you got your cards mixed up because you would have to start all over again; any card out of its proper sequence would stop the drawing. The whole process took way too much time for the end result, but little did any of them know that computer-aided drafting would be the future of the profession.

Courses in the final year included building construction, legal aspects of the profession, urban planning, sketching, drafting, design, and model building. Each student in the final class had to pick a specific building project, design it, build a model, and then present it to the teaching staff and some of the local architects who acted as critics. Lonnie picked a concert hall for his project. The site he chose was the northeast corner of Sackville and Brunswick, where currently a car dealership existed. Slope issues and access for parking were considered potential problems; however close to the city core was the best for this type of project. Parking was accommodated via Market Street into a parking garage, which was on the lowest level of his design. From there patrons would take the escalator or elevator to the main lobby. Of course, all the final projects were hypothetical, since no contracts were given for the projects.

Another professor was very helpful for Lonnie, and that was Ojars Biscaps. He helped with several questionable items in Lonnie's concept for the concert hall, plus he provided responses that made Lonnie re-think the overall design. The end result was a revised conceptual design for the building.

Around this time the Metropolitan Area Planning Commission (MAPC) had been established to make plans for the future development of the Halifax and Dartmouth area. They had constructed a model of the downtown of Halifax on a scale of one inch equal to forty feet. Lonnie became aware of this model and contacted MAPC to see if he could use it for his final project. Fortunately they had no problem with him using it for pictures, which was the intent of the model in the first place. The model could be taken apart block-by-block and building-by-building so Lonnie constructed a model of his concert hall project to fit in the area of the current car dealership. Then he had photos taken and blown up to a size of three feet by four feet to illustrate his conceptual project within the city. Overall it looked like his project was part of the MAPC model, and the final presentation went very well.

CHAPTER 24

Graduation day, in May of 1971 was very special. Lonnie was the first Donaldson on his side of the family tree to graduate from university. Sadly, his parents were not able to be there, but Robert, Mary, Margret, and her boyfriend Ronald, plus Patricia and her family, were able to attend the ceremonies. They were held on-campus in the Sexton Gymnasium and it was a fine spring day. After graduation, both families went back to Robert and Mary's place on Beech Street for sandwiches, coffee, tea, and sweets from the French Pastry on Quinpool Road. Lonnie was pleased with the family celebrating his accomplishments.

Robert and Mary were very proud of their adopted children. Margie had a good job in Truro with the Royal Bank and Lonnie had just graduated with a degree in architecture. They both knew that these young people were on the road to a successful life and they would not have to worry about them. Lonnie, Patricia, Margie, and Ronald spent some time together talking about their futures. Ronald knew he would be staying with Richard's Pharmacy as his father was looking forward to retirement. Margie was quite content with the Royal Bank, but when they got married and started a family, she planned to be a stay at home mom.

Shortly after graduation that spring, the Nova Scotia Association of Architects invited Lonnie and the other graduates of 1971 to meet at the Henry House restaurant on Barrington Street. When everyone was assembled and had dined, the president of the NSAA, George Ripley, welcomed each of them to the profession of architecture. George described the process to become registered with the association and encouraged each of them to be sure they could find employment that would allow them to gain the required experience to apply for membership. He said that two years of working with a registered architect who would sign off on the experience was the main requirement to be able to apply for membership.

Then George presented all the graduates with the customary silver ring which had the year of graduation and their initials engraved on the inside and was worn on the right hand pinky finger. At that time each of the seven schools of architecture across Canada had silver rings for graduates, but each school's rings were slightly different so you could recognize from which school they had graduated. Sometimes people would think that Lonnie was an engineer, so he would very quickly set them straight: engineers had rings of steel and architects had rings of sterling silver.

Lonnie looked forward to becoming a member of the NSAA and a registered architect. But first he had to put in his time working under an architect's guidance with an architectural firm. He began his search for work in his chosen profession.

CHAPTER 25

It was in 1969 that Margie had met Robert Richard from Truro; he had studied pharmacy at Dalhousie and was in the process of taking over the family drug store on Prince Street. They had met when she was first working at the Royal Bank on Quinpool Road. Since he had banked with the Royal Bank in Truro he dealt with the one on Quinpool Road when he was studying at Dalhousie. His last name was one that could have been a first name. His nickname was double R. They dated a bit while he was studying in Halifax and there seemed to be some magnetism between them. Margie had brought him home previously to meet Robert and Mary and they thought he was a nice young man.

Margie was considering moving away from Halifax and was thinking that Truro might be a good location. Close to Halifax if need be, yet far enough away. She may have also been thinking of Ronald, but kept her thoughts to herself. She requested and got a transfer to the Royal Bank in Truro on Esplanade Street in 1970 and found a basement apartment that suited her needs; the price was very reasonable, and close to work.

Of course, Ronald was pleased that she was nearby and they began dating on a regular basis with many a walk in Victoria Park. It was not long after that he proposed, on one of the many walks in Victoria Park by the falls, and she accepted. The wedding was planned for the following spring.

The wedding took place at Bethany United Church during the month of July in 1971. The reception was set for the

Waegwoltic Club, on the Northwest Arm. The catering service was provided by Lohnes' Restaurant. It had rained heavily at the beginning of the service but stopped midway and the sun was shining when the service was finished. It was a beautiful day and several boats were sailing in the North West Arm. The guests enjoyed the reception, the meal, and all the stories. There were lots of laughs and everyone had a good time. Ronald's best man told some interesting stories about Ronald in his youth, some that Margie did not know about. Margie did wish her parents could have been there, but that was out of the question. Robert and Mary both enjoyed sitting with Ronald's parents and sharing stories about each of the families.

Lonnie and Patricia sat together during the service and at the reception. Since Lonnie had graduated from architecture, he was thinking that perhaps it may be the time for them to get married. They both liked Bethany United Church and discussed that it would be a good place for their marriage when the time came along. But they were not in a rush; for the moment their careers were on the top of their list of things to accomplish before marriage.

Ronald found a few moments to come and sit with Lonnie and Patricia. He specifically wanted to speak to Lonnie, for when the time came he wanted to do some renovations to the family drugstore in Truro. He also mentioned that he wanted Lonnie to design a new home for him and Margie in a few years, at the time when they planned to start a family. Lonnie was more than pleased that Ronald was seeking out his professional services in advance. Lonnie logged that away until Ronald and Margie were ready

Ronald and Margie left the reception and drove to St. Andrew's, New Brunswick that evening and stayed at the Algonquin by the Sea Hotel. The next day they drove to Maine and did some shopping at L.L. Bean in Freeport before heading down Interstate 95 to Boston for a few days. They returned to Truro on the following weekend. They had found a nice apartment in an older home on Smith Avenue and settled in to married life.

CHAPTER 26

The task of finding a job in architecture for Lonnie did not bode well. There was a downturn in the economy and most of the local architectural firms were not hiring at the moment. However, the Federal Government was hiring people for a study of the existing post offices in Nova Scotia and Lonnie was able to get hired as part of the team. Lonnie was interviewed on the eighth of June, accepted, and the next day he was paired with a mechanical engineer. Their job was to travel around Nova Scotia and prepare reports on the current status of postal buildings around the province. It was not an exciting job but it helped pay the bills. He was part of four two-man teams and they finished three quarters of the province that first summer. During that time Lonnie called the MAPC office looking for work. He would call once or twice a week until finally the person in charge said, "You are going to keep calling until I hire you," to which Lonnie replied "Yes, I am very interested in what you are trying to accomplish." Shortly afterwards, in September, Lonnie was employed with MAPC.

MAPC was tasked with preparing a municipal development plan for the Halifax and Dartmouth metropolitan area. The purpose was to determine the best areas to develop for housing, what roads were needed and where, and what services would be required. Where should industrial sites, parklands, commercial sites, railways, sewer and water services, and treatment plants be located. A map of the metropolitan area was divided into a nine-acre grid; vegetation, depth to bedrock, type of bedrock, soil type, ease of excavation, slope, marshes, bogs, and water courses were each evaluated to determine the best areas for development in the metropolitan area.

The findings resulted in informed decisions. For example, the best area for housing development was Cole Harbour compared to Spryfield. The estimated cost to develop land in Cole Harbour at that time was fifteen thousand dollars per acre and in Spryfield it was thirty-six thousand dollars per acre. The difference was due to the amount of granite rock in the Spryfield area as opposed to the clay soil in the Cole Harbour area. The cost estimates took into account excavation costs, servicing costs, road construction, and the like.

Another proposed development location under consideration was for an industrial park. Industrial parks require good transportation systems, access via road and rail, sewer, water, and electrical services. The Burnside area on the Dartmouth side of the harbor scored the best for this type of development. Halifax was concerned that they would not have an industrial park and the group was tasked with finding a suitable site on the Halifax side of the Harbor. Bayers Lake was selected as it had the services required. The MAPC experience was one that Lonnie would never forget.

Following MAPC, Lonnie worked for a short time with the Provincial Community Planning Department. While there he was involved in the preparation of Municipal Development Plans for several communities. Then he was hired by a local consulting firm to continue with planning different types of projects, such as the preparation of municipal development plans for various communities and towns around the Maritimes.

CHAPTER 27

Lonnie was being troubled by a tooth, a back molar, and so he made an appointment with his dentist. The dentist carried out a complete investigation and found that the molar required a small filling. His gum was frozen and the dentist drilled out the small cavity and filled the tooth.

During his visit to the dentist the subject of flying came up since Lonnie noticed a picture of a plane on the wall. His dentist, Chris Gregoire, was himself a pilot and offered to take Lonnie up flying with him. Lonnie had an interest in flying but really never gave it a second thought. Chris loved flying and would go at the drop of a hat and liked to take others with him. So the Saturday following his dental appointment Lonnie found himself at the Halifax Flying Club at Halifax International Airport, watching Chris walking around a plane and rubbing his fingers on the propeller and the wings, checking the oil, fuel, and air in the tires. Then it was time for Lonnie to walk out to the plane and climb in the co-pilot seat next to Chris. Chris explained as much as he could about flying, and what to expect as they taxied to the active runway. Once they were given clearance from the control tower they taxied to the end of runway 06 and took off.

Lonnie was excited and enjoyed every minute of their hour flight around Halifax, Sambro, St. Margret's Bay, and Peggy's Cove. Lonnie noticed that the takeoff was very smooth and so was the landing. After the flight he discussed with Chris what was involved to obtain a flying license. Lonnie was so excited that on his way home, when he stopped to tell Patricia, she could hardly get him to slow down. Lonnie and Patricia discussed the possibility of him taking the flying course. Patricia was smart enough not to be negative and gave him her blessing. She was not sure that he would carry through with training. Lonnie also discussed this with Robert, he was also not sure it was a good idea, but caved to Lonnie's excitement.

And so Lonnie registered at the Halifax Flying Club for flying lessons. When his manager of the consulting firm heard about Lonnie taking flying lessons he encouraged him to go out early in the morning and take the required lessons before coming to work. This was a way to expedite the process of acquiring his license.

One day he was practicing slow flight. The object being to find the lowest speed obtainable while maintaining the same elevation. As he kept reducing speed the altimeter was showing he was still climbing. It was when he had the throttle completely off, he realized that he was caught in a thermal, something that glider pilots search for. That was an interesting experience.

The end result for Lonnie, after obtaining his flying license, was flying the company staff around the Maritimes to various jobs that the company was engaged in. This increased the number of hours and experience for Lonnie, something that would be of value for future work. To get to the airport they used a limo service and their favorite driver was Brenda Martin. Brenda was a redhead from Cape Breton and always had a quick comeback, but she was very dependable. Lonnie made sure he got her business card for future reference.

CHAPTER 28

Lonnie and Patricia had been dating for over nine years now. On one of their outings to Crystal Crescent Beach, in early July of 1973, Lonnie got down on one knee on the beach and proposed. He didn't have the money for an engagement ring, but he did have his mother's diamond engagement ring. Patricia was not only excited about marriage, but also moved by the thought behind his mother's ring. She couldn't wait to show her parents when they got back home.

The drive back to Halifax was warm with excitement. They talked about where they would live and children and when that would happen. Both wanted children, but it was agreed that they had to be financially secure before they should consider starting a family. Shortly afterwards, when they arrived on Robert Murphy Drive, Patricia dashed out of the car quickly, and ran inside the house to show her parents her engagement ring. Her parents were not shocked; they were just wondering when this would happen. Both liked Lonnie and were pleased to have him becoming their son-in-law. Jasper was also happy for his sister. Roger invited Lonnie in for a celebration drink of scotch and Gail and Patricia started discussing plans for the wedding.

Lonnie and Patricia had discussed eloping but both wanted more to remember than just a quick marriage. They also wanted both their families involved to share their special day. Lonnie wanted Michael to be his best man and Patricia wanted her friend from Westmount Junior High School, Patsy Jennings, to be her maid of honor.

Robert and Mary were also excited about the upcoming nuptials and were available to help organize the wedding. They met with Roger and Gail to assist with the planning. Both families worked well together, enjoyed each other's company, and were happy for both of them. Mary and Gail met to discuss the details of the special day.

Since the engagement, Lonnie had found an apartment on South Street that was close to work for him and close to the hospital for Patricia. And it had a lovely view of Holy Cross Cemetery. Lonnie moved in the first of September and Patricia helped with the furniture layout, what little they had at that time. New furniture would be in the future. For a start it was a comfortable location and the price fit their pocketbooks.

CHAPTER 29

Bethany United Church by the Armdale rotary was chosen as the location for the ceremony. Since the wedding was scheduled for September of that year, plans were put together hastily. There was no reason to wait and no reason not to proceed. Patricia already knew who her bridesmaids would be and Lonnie knew that his best man would be Michael and his three other friends from high school: Skip, Bob, and Ken. The date was set for Saturday, September fifteenth. Both Lonnie and Patricia were excited and hopefully Lonnie would remember the date in the coming years.

The ceremony went as planned. Both bride and groom were lovely and their smiles were a testament to their love for each other, a love that had grown very strong over many years. Patricia looked wonderful in her white wedding dress and long train. Her cousin's niece was the ring bearer. Although Michael was clean shaven, his suit looked a little rough around the edges and his shoes were not polished to a high shine; in fact, they had a few scuff marks on them. Lonnie was a little more than concerned about his best man, but there was not much that he could do at that point.

The reception was held at Ashburn Golf and Country Club. Several club staff congratulated both Lonnie and Patricia. Those in attendance had a wonderful meal of lamb chops with mint jelly, mini potatoes and green beans, followed by a chocolate brownie, vanilla ice cream, and chocolate sauce.

Michael spoke about their childhood together on the LaHave River, for he was not familiar with what happened after Lonnie moved to Halifax. There were some good laughs and in particular about Lonnie's first bike riding lesson and how he avoided being hit by a car by driving into the ditch; that brought several more laughs. Then he spoke about some of the trouble they used to get into, especially the fire that they had set which resulted in fire trucks and next the police arriving at their doors. Michael drifted off a bit when speaking about Lonnie learning how to shoot a .22 rifle and how he was a much better marksman. Lonnie was getting a little nervous as Michael began to talk about himself and his sales successes. Those in attendance were not sure why this was even part of the discussion. Lonnie had to politely cut him off and he finished by congratulating them both and wishing them the best for a long and happy marriage. At that point Lonnie began to relax somewhat.

Patricia's friend Patsy spoke about their childhood days from grade seven at Westmount Junior High School to their years at Queen Elizabeth High School. She went on to say that Patricia was a bit of a sport person in terms of playing baseball, basketball, volleyball, and soccer. Pearl Williams was also one of the bridesmaids but she was not given an opportunity to speak, which was probably a good thing; she might have had a few good stories about Digby. She was now living in Halifax and going to Saint Mary's for a degree in education.

It was an enjoyable afternoon for everyone there. Lonnie was now driving a 1966 Volvo sedan and he had it serviced before the ceremony in preparation for their honeymoon. After they left the reception, they drove to the Nova Scotian Hotel; they had a room booked on the top floor that overlooked Halifax Harbour for that evening. The Queen Mary cruise ship was visible at dock. While not the first time for them, it was the first time that it was technically legal. They both enjoyed each other and both responded to sexual advances with a strong appetite. Soon afterwards they fell into a deep sleep in each other's arms.

In the morning they showered, dressed, and went down to the dining room for breakfast. After breakfast they retrieved their luggage, checked out, and headed to Cape Breton to Ingonish Beech Lodge for a few days of relaxation and golf at Highland Links Golf Course, a Stanley Thompson design that followed the river up for nine holes and then down the river for nine holes. It was a mecca for all golfers. It was early fall and the leaves were starting to change color. The walk on the course was magnificent. They shared lots of laughs, lost a few balls, and saw foxes, moose, and eagles. You had to be vigilant so that one of the foxes didn't steal your golf ball.

They packed up on Thursday morning and checked out. Next they drove around the Cabot Trail to Cheticamp. The scenery was spectacular. There they had booked a cabin overlooking the ocean for a few days and had reservations for some golf at Le Portage Golf Club, one of the hidden secrets of golfing in Cape Breton. They played that afternoon and later, while sitting on the deck of their cabin enjoying a glass of Pinot Grigio, they watched a pod of whales offshore going south along the coast. That night they dined on crab legs with potato salad at the Le Gabriel Restaurant & Lounge and of course had some more wine.

After a few days of golf and fine dining it was time to head back to their apartment and start their new life together. The drive to Halifax was through a rainstorm most of the way back, but the car got washed.

CHAPTER 30

While the planning experience which Lonnie had gained provided an excellent background for him in the field of urban planning, it did not include the experience required to become a registered architect. After a few years with the consulting firm, in 1974 Lonnie joined another architect in Halifax who had a small practice both in Halifax and Charlottetown, Prince Edward Island. His name was David Mathers. Lonnie and David met during an architect's baseball game that was organized by the NSAA that he was invited to as an up-and-coming architect.

David's Halifax office was located on the corner of Spring Garden Road and Brunswick Street, at the north-west corner, on the second floor in a three-story building with a brick facade. It was a great location, close to lots of restaurants, the School of Architecture, the Halifax Library, and Bud the Spud French fry wagon which arrived every at noontime in front of the library.

In the fall of 1976, after gaining experience with David, and David signing his record book, Lonnie became licensed to practice Architecture in Nova Scotia. As a member of the Nova Scotia Association of Architects (NSAA), the annual fees also included membership in the Royal Architectural Institute of Canada (RAIC). His partner David decided to continue with his work in Prince Edward Island so Lonnie took over the Nova Scotia practice in 1978.

Work was increasing, so he had to find staff to help; first another partner, then a secretary, then architects and draftsmen. Since he was now a member of the NSAA, Lonnie could attend the annual general meeting held each spring. At one such meeting in the early eighties he met an architect named Dennis Manning.

Dennis was not happy with his current employment and he and Lonnie discussed a partnership. Dennis felt that he was not given the freedom to design larger projects with the firm where he was currently employed and was looking for an opportunity to expand his expertise. Plus he did not like the work that his current firm was doing; he felt that they could be more inventive with their projects and not just build the same type of buildings over and over again. In his opinion he would not get anywhere with that firm. It was not long after that meeting that Lonnie and Dennis formed Donaldson and Manning Architects.

Dennis had graduated from the University of Manitoba and had ended up in Halifax when he was touring Canada after graduating. He had found architectural work with a firm in Halifax and later became registered with the NSAA. Soon he was very comfortable in Halifax and had met Sandra, his future wife, on a visit to the Art Gallery of Nova Scotia. They had discussed a few of the local paintings together and found that they had a lot in common. There was one artist that they particularly liked and that was Bill DeGarth; his scenes around Peggy's Cove were wonderful. They dated and made some trips to Peggy's Cove to visit the DeGarth studio, plus to walk around the famous lighthouse. Sandra and Dennis became very intrigued with each other and soon took up residence together. Marriage followed a few years later.

Donaldson and Manning's first office space was in the former Halifax Infirmary building on Barrington Street near Blower Street. It was not great, but suitable for a short time. Both Lonnie and Dennis had drafting tables. They purchased an IBM electric typewriter for letters and contract documents. While they preferred to visit clients in their own offices, clients would occasionally come to their small office, so a meeting area was set aside. The space was not large, but adequate at that time. It was time to think about expanding: first a draftsman, then a second draftsman, then an architect, then a secretary/receptionist, and then new office space.

One of the first projects of note was a renovation of Lonnie's brother-in-law's drugstore in Truro. Ronald had wanted to modernize his family business as it had been the same space for over forty years. Since Ronald's father had retired and Ronald was now in charge of the business he wanted to upgrade the store to today's standards. Lonnie and Dennis conceptualized several ideas before settling on what the design for the store should be and after a meeting with Ronald to present the ideas, Ronald accepted the conceptual design and so Lonnie and Dennis began the next stage of finalizing the design and the preparation of the final contract documents. Ronald had a contractor friend that after studying the drawings gave Ronald a fair price for the renovations and the work proceeded without any difficulty. The end result was a modern store interior and storefront which was well received in the town.

CHAPTER 31

The office was expanding and the work continued to flow in and around the Maritimes. The fact that Lonnie had a flying license enabled him and staff, when required, to get to distant projects quickly. The Halifax Flying Club rental of planes was very reasonable at first, since they only charged for flying time recorded. Then they started to charge for the amount of time away. At that point and since the business was doing very well, Lonnie with three other pilots purchased a 1953 Piper Saratoga II, which, along with the pilot, would hold an additional three staff members, when required on projects. In order to do that he had to take some funds from his account that was set up after his parent's death. The plane was completely airworthy; airtime and the maintenance required for an aircraft were followed by the book religiously. Failure to follow the maintenance manual could have serious consequences if a problem occurred. While flying, it was not possible to pull over to locate a problem. The four owners shared the expenses equally based on the amount of hours flown monthly and had no trouble adjusting flying times for seldom did any of them want the plane at the same time.

Almost all major and some minor locations in the Maritimes had a landing strip of some sort, either paved or not paved, resulting in considerable savings in travel time and dollars spent, since driving a vehicle, meals, and accommodation for staff to get to project sites were all avoided. Lonnie and his flying partners kept the plane in a rented hangar at the Halifax International Airport. Company projects helped with his portion of the payments for the hangar rental.

Now it was time to move the office. Through a friend—Sandy Roman from Domus Realty—Lonnie and Dennis searched for a suitable building to purchase for office space. They found one on Windsor Street, in Halifax. Both Lonnie and Dennis worked on some minor renovations to get the space ready to serve for an architect's office. They painted the building throughout and replaced the roof shingles. To distinguish their office from the other buildings on the street they installed a round eight-foot diameter window on the front elevation. They moved in early September 1981.

Additional staff was required and the first to be hired was a receptionist by the name of Kathy Wilcox. Kathy turned out to be quite the girl Friday: she could type specifications, letters, organize files, do basic accounting, answer the phone, and handle product salesmen who made the un-expected visits to the office.

Kathy was followed by the addition of a graduate architect and two draftsmen. The graduate architect's name was Brad McPhee and the initial feelings from the first interview were that he would fit in very well with the goals and objectives of the firm. The draftsmen were Penny Lane and Roger MacKenzie. Both were keen to be employed and proficient with AutoCAD. Since 1971 AutoCAD had progressed very rapidly to the point of being a computer program and could be used with any laptop or desk top computer.

The firm purchased the required AutoCAD license for the draftsmen and soon drawings were being produced quickly and accurately. The fact that the drawings could be forwarded by email to the mechanical and electrical engineers and other sub consultants as a base for their work helped to expedite the projects. While the firm also had a fax machine it was used mainly for letters and other matters which required the sharing of printed information.

When the drawings were completed to the satisfaction of each professional on the project they were sent to Norman Wade Company for reproduction and printing of the documents, both drawings and specifications. Norman Wade Company kept the originals for additional printing as needed during the bidding period of the project.

One of the first projects to be designed and printed with the new AutoCAD license was a new home for Margie and Ronald in Truro. They had purchased a waterfront lot on Shortts Lake, with a southern exposure, and a short distance from Truro. It was good to use a small project to start with AutoCAD to be sure that system worked as intended.

While Lonnie was in charge of the design on this project, Dennis gave him some good ideas for the new home. Lonnie and Ronald played a few games of golf at the Truro Golf and Country Club and Lonnie had Ronald's full attention for four hours to discuss possible things about the new home. He also met with Margie to get her ideas for the house. Both Margie and Ronald were very pleased with the design and the construction process and very pleased that it was completed within the budget they had available. Lonnie made several site visits during the construction period to make sure the contractor was following the contract documents. Margie and Ronald were looking forward to moving into their new home. Lonnie and Patricia along with Dennis and Sandra were invited to the house warming celebration that fall.

CHAPTER 32

Patricia got pregnant. It was not intended, but it happened. It must have been the long weekend that they spent at Milford House, near Annapolis Royal the previous July. They had driven down on a Friday evening after they left work and enjoyed a quiet weekend just by themselves. Over the weekend they played a few games of golf at Digby Pines Golf Course, another Stanley Thompson Golf Course, and only a short drive away. On the way back from the golf course they dropped in on Pearl's parents in Bear River for a short visit. They also got to enjoy some pleasant evenings canoeing the lakes around the area and after dining in the main lodge they spent time by the fireplace reading and relaxing (well maybe not relaxing the total time they were away).

Patricia had been feeling tired and sleepy more than usual and then she did not have her regular period. So they picked up a pregnancy test kit from the Shopper's Drugstore. Sure enough, it was positive. So they made an appointment with her doctor for a proper checkup. After the checkup the doctor confirmed that she was indeed pregnant.

They had been talking about starting a family, but now changes would have to be made. The one-bedroom apartment was no longer suitable and so they began looking around for a larger one. After another visit to the doctor and an ultrasound the doctor advised them that there were two heartbeats, not just one. They were shocked to find out that they would be having twins. They had quite the laugh over that. At this point they had not said anything to Patricia's parents or to Robert and Mary; they wanted to wait to see how the pregnancy was developing first and that Patricia would be able to cope with the upcoming changes.

After a few visits to the doctor and all was well and the fact that Patricia began to show they agreed it was time to tell their parents. They invited Robert, Mary, Roger, and Gail to their apartment for a bar-b-que. Mary was the first to notice that Patricia seemed to be gaining a little weight and had a questioning look on her face when Lonnie indicated that he wished to make an announcement. Lonnie started by saying that his family would be expanding in about seven months. That brought congratulations from both families. Then he mentioned that they were having twins. Next he brought out the ultrasound picture to show each of them.

The families thought that it would be an interesting change for everyone. Robert and Mary were excited for them and so were Roger and Gail. Both families agreed to babysit when needed. After the bar-b-que was over they both were relieved that their news was very well received by everyone. They had to prepare for the changes that were about to unfold.

They discussed how the birth of two was going to change their daily lifestyle, and what they needed for the twins in terms of furnishings. In September they found another apartment with an extra bedroom on Pepperell Street, close to the Halifax Commons and the Halifax Infirmary. The Commons would be a great spot for walking the twins. After one of the later visits to the doctor they found out by ultrasound that one was a boy and one was a girl. The new apartment would suffice until the twins got old enough that separate bedrooms were required. In the meantime, they ordered both pink and blue bassinets.

CHAPTER 33

The pregnancy went well. Patricia did have cravings for chocolate and Kalamata olives but those were easy items to get. Well, she was eating for three. Funny she didn't want ice cream. The first few months that fall, the pregnancy was not an issue, however around Christmas that year she was having trouble getting comfortable sleeping at night. The ultrasounds continued to show that both twins were growing at a healthy rate and that there was no cause for concern. Her doctor suggested that perhaps near the birth date that it would be best if she was in the hospital to ensure that if problems arose they could be taken care of quickly.

By the first of March she was very uncomfortable and her doctor strongly suggested that she go to the hospital and she, with the assistance of Lonnie, checked in on March second. Now whenever there was a concern she was in a place where care was immediate. Lonnie could also rest a little easier and spend a few more hours at the office.

On March twelfth Lonnie was with Patricia at the hospital when her water broke at seven fifty-three p.m. Her doctor was called immediately and he was only forty-five minutes away. The nurses made her as comfortable as they could. She did not want an epidural, regardless of her discomfort. Lonnie was able to sit with her in the delivery room and he held her left hand. The doctor arrived and all the hospital staff prepared for the birthing. While the twins were on their way they were quite comfortable in the womb for a few more hours. Contractions had not yet started.

In the wee hours of March thirteenth, the contractions began in earnest and the doctor was called back to the delivery room. A few words uttered by Patricia, during the birth, would not be heard during any sermon on a given Sunday. Both babies were delivered safely, and those cries heard would not be the last in the Donaldson household. It was quite the picture to see Patricia with a baby in each arm. The smile on her face was wider than the Bay of Fundy. Ben and Chloe were the names given. Benjamin Ross was born two minutes before Chloe Jeanette.

After the birthing Patricia was moved to another room where she quickly fell asleep. Both the babies were bundled and asleep in the nursery. Lonnie was wide awake and not sure what to do so he called Robert and Mary to tell them the news and then he called Patricia's parents. While both were awoken in the early hours, both forgave Lonnie's excitement and were pleased that he called.

Lonnie and Patricia did not get much sleep for a few months with feedings and diaper changing occurring at all hours. But they didn't complain; they enjoyed their new family. Lonnie, when he could, would do some office work at home so that he didn't fall too far behind with his part of the business. Dennis, as a father before Lonnie, understood what his partner was dealing with.

One weekend Lonnie and Patricia placed the twins in their car seats and drove up to Shortts Lake to visit Margie and Ronald. They were happy to see them and the twins and did comment that their house had performed very well mechanically and that they enjoyed living on the lake. Margie prepared a lunch of sandwiches and a small salad. While

Lonnie and Patricia were eating Margie was feeding one of the twins and Ronald was feeding the other.

Patricia stayed home with the twins for almost a year before she decided that it was time to go back to work. There was a day care close to the apartment on Pepperell Street and both Lonnie and Patricia were satisfied with the fees, and the care provided. Patricia enrolled them both in Sunshine Pre-School. Soon they were walking, talking, and getting into all kinds of mischief.

CHAPTER 34

Work in the firm continued to flow. Their reputation was growing around the Maritimes. That fall they actually got invited to submit a proposal for a golf course clubhouse located at the Sugarloaf Ski Hill in Maine, USA. Lonnie and Dennis flew down for a site visit in late September to get an idea of the lay of the land and also to meet with some members of the design review committee. They had to make arrangements with USA Customs to meet them at a designated airport to clear them for entry in the United States. Bangor International Airport was designated as the point of entry and customs clearance was a formality. From there they continued the short flight to Sugarloaf. There was a small grass runway in the Carrabassett Valley and they landed there close to noon and were met by some members of the design committee who drove them to the intended project site at the ski hill.

The design review committee was impressed that they were taking the time to make a site visit before the project was even awarded. Lonnie explained that it was the best way to see what they were getting themselves into before submitting a proposal. Some of the other firms invited did not take the time for a site visit, just made their submissions based on the original proposal call documents. The design committee had prepared a very detailed space program and they went over all the details with Lonnie and Dennis.

The meeting lasted a few hours and it was dusk when they returned to the airfield for the trip home. Lonnie had taken night endorsement during his flying lessons which enabled him to fly legally at night. They had a pleasant flight back to Halifax. The sky was so clear that the stars were spectacular that evening. Again they had to go through customs at Halifax International Airport. That was an easy process since they did not have anything to declare. Brenda, who was always dependable, met them at the hanger where the plane was stored, when they arrived and she drove them back to the office to get their own vehicles.

The rest of the next week Lonnie and Dennis worked together to prepare the proposal for the clubhouse project. They spent a few nights after normal working hours putting their proposal together. They both knew that the project itself would require the basic design process, that was a given. They brainstormed about what might set their project design apart from the other forthcoming proposals. Lonnie poured a few fingers of scotch for both of them. Dennis, while sipping his drink mentioned that when the golf course was being used the ski hill would be closed so perhaps they would not need to construct a parking lot if they could share the one currently on the ski hill. Also, perhaps the golf course clubhouse could be used for fine dining by the skiers when the golf course was closed. Both of those items were not mentioned in the competition package and that may give them an advantage with their proposal. As a way for the golf course clubhouse project to get approval from the ski hill operators to use their parking lot perhaps the golf clubhouse project could pave the parking area on the ski hill. They prepared their proposal with these ideas in mind and fully described them in their proposal documents.

When their proposal and the schematic drawings were completed they had several copies printed and sent to them by air mail along with their company brochure. After a few weeks went by they received a phone call from the chairman of the design review committee that they were going to be awarded the project. Both Lonnie and Dennis were excited and very pleased with this news and began to get staff in line. This was their first international project.

The review committee agreed that the design was extremely good and went beyond their initial space program, one of the reasons they were awarded the contract. This was the first international project for Donaldson and Matheson. They had to get a license to practice architecture in Maine, which, with the support of the design review committee, was not an issue.

After they won the design competition, and the preliminary design was completed, Dennis mailed the drawings to the design review committee for any further comments. Then he and Lonnie flew down to Maine again to meet with the design review committee to discuss any final items in regards to the project with them. This time they flew down early in the morning and were back in Halifax by early evening. Email was also a means to deliver notes or specific specification items to the design committee. Not only was the delivery quick, so was the response, which helped to move the project forward.

When the design was finalized and approved by the design review committee, Dennis orchestrated the staff to put a rush on the construction documents. He received and met all the necessary requirements for the building codes applicable to Maine. It was interesting to note how the building codes varied between different jurisdictions. After several reviews by senior staff the drawings and specifications were stamped and then forwarded to the Sugarloaf Development Committee for printing and distribution through the Maine Construction Association. From there, contractors that were interested in bidding on the project, placed a deposit on each set of drawings, and the construction documents they needed for their bid purposes. Several respectable contractors took out the documents.

CHAPTER 35

Contractor questions on the bid documents were minimal and the bids received were within a reasonable range, just two percent above the initial project budget. The additional paving of the ski hill parking area was the main reason for the additional cost. The design committee was pleased and the low bidder was a contractor from Bigelow Contracting, just down the road from the ski hill. Construction was scheduled to start in late March after the ski hill closed. Dennis had sought out a local architectural firm in Bangor to be their eyes and ears during the construction period when Lonnie was not available for site visits. The firm they planned to work with was Avery Architects, a one man practice but with twenty-five years of experience of working in this area of Maine. Lonnie and Dennis were of the opinion that working with local expertise was far better than stepping on toes in that industry.

Lonnie flew down to Sugarloaf to meet with Harry Walsh, the owner of Bigelow Contracting. Harry was a young man but very excited about the contract his firm had just won. He and Lonnie hit it off right from the start. They met at Harry's office in Bigelow along with the chair of the design review committee, Ralph Waters. Harry had some questions about some of the details and after some discussion with Lonnie his concerns were put to rest. Harry and his family were skiers and he knew most of the ski hill management so he had a direct line of communication in case any issues in regards to the ski hill arose during construction.

Harry planned to begin construction shortly after the ski hill closed for the season at the end of March. His first phase of the construction was to excavate for the foundation and have it poured, cured, and then the forms could be removed. Next he planned to backfill the foundation and then complete all the paving of the parking lot for the project by sometime in June. That way he could keep the site clean of mud when he started to prepare the main floor of the golf clubhouse, plus it gave him a clean area to store the lumber and other supplies required for the building. He went on to say that he would not have the clubhouse completed until the following year as the construction period would take a good twelve months. Lonnie was not surprised nor was Ralph Waters.

Harry was familiar with Avery Architects as they had worked on several projects previously. So there were no foreseen obstacles apparent at this time. Lonnie was a phone call away and if needed on site Harry promised that he would give him a few days' notice before he wanted him and Lonnie would fly down.

The construction phase went as expected, no major issues. Only once did Lonnie have to make an emergency inspection since Avery Architects were not available at that time. There were a few small change orders, but also some credits were found and the project moved along very well.

The clubhouse was designed with post and beam as the main structural elements and they were to be visible on the interior of the building. Dennis had investigated the availability of large lumber suitable for this project even before he started his initial design. Harry was one of the well know contractors of heavy timber construction in Maine—perhaps that was why he was the low bidder. Being on Sugarloaf Mountain, the visual aspects of the building were important to the overall appearance of the project.

Working across international borders was an interesting experience for both Lonnie and Dennis but there were no major issues as long as they complied with the required customs clearances. After several trips they both became well-known with the customs officers and crossing the border became a formality.

The following year when the project was finished Lonnie, Patricia, Dennis, and Sandra flew down to Sugarloaf for the grand opening of the Sugarloaf Mountain Golf Course clubhouse. They cleared customs in Bangor as usual and then flew on to the runway in the Carrabasset Valley where there were met by Harry Walsh and his wife, Ester, who drove them to the clubhouse. The opening ceremonies went very well and Dennis was asked to say a few words as his design was greatly appreciated by those in attendance. Dennis was encouraged by some of the dignitaries to enter this project for the upcoming USA Architectural Design Awards. Dennis said he would give that some consideration.

The project was a large success for Donaldson and Manning and they started to get invited on other projects both in Canada and the USA.

CHAPTER 36

In 1985 Lonnie and Patricia decided that perhaps it was time to think of a family home, a place where the twins could grow up before they ventured out on their own. Lonnie was aware of an available lot on Chain Rock Drive, near Point Pleasant Park, a wonderful location in the city, and the park made it extra special. Plus there was an elementary school nearby. They discussed the idea of living there and both agreed, so Lonnie started the process of purchasing the lot. He was able to knock the price down a few thousand dollars and the deal was made. They took ownership on November twentieth, 1985 and Lonnie began sketches of possible home designs while he was home with the family and the twins were not taking up his time.

Of course Patricia had her say in what she wanted for the home. Lonnie built a model out of cardboard, so that she could get an idea of what the home would look like. Maybe a bit ahead of its time, but they both agreed that they didn't want separate rooms for each activity. So the living, dining, and kitchen were accommodated in one large space on the main floor. The basement included a recreation room, and a TV theater room with theater seating. Lonnie and Patricia hoped that their kids would bring their friends home to their place, so they would know where they were most of the time. Since the lot was sloped, the recreation room had its own at-grade entrance and the kids could come and go when they pleased, after they told their parents where they were going.

Lonnie called his old friend Garth Redding from his Redding Construction days to see if Garth was able to construct their home. While Garth did have some projects on the go at the moment he was more than pleased to work with Lonnie to build their home. After Garth prepared cost estimates from the drawings, he presented his price and Lonnie gave him the go ahead for construction. Garth did advise that he could not start the work until early May but that he should have it completed by the end of September.

The house did not go over budget by very much. There were just a few last minute additions which created some extra costs. The construction went pretty much as planned (after all, it was construction). They moved in on Sunday, October fifth, 1986, on Alexander Keith's birthday as a matter of fact.

On the main floor there were four bedrooms, one for Lonnie and Patricia, one for Ben, one for Chloe and a spare when needed, which also doubled as a study for Patricia. The garage was fitted out as a workshop where Lonnie could use some of the skills he developed when being trained by Arthur Whynott. He found that working with wood was a good way to spend his spare time, when he could find some.

The exterior of the home was clad in a combination of brick and Dryvit. Dryvit was the trade name for a type of stucco. The brick was from L. E. Shaw of Lantz and the Dryvit came from Nutech Specialty Products Limited, of Burnside. The patio at the back of the home faced south and was of Folly Lake aggregate, so maintenance was minimal. A roof extended over part of the patio for some protection when using the bar-b-que in the rain. There were steps down to the lower lever for the at-grade entrance. The landscaping was also minimal: no grass, just shrubs and low maintenance ground covers. Lonnie hated mowing grass, something he considered a complete waste of time, so he made sure he would not have that as a maintenance issue.

Because they liked the daycare that the twins were registered with, they kept them there after the house was completed. They would soon be going to primary school so no need to change at this time. In addition Patricia was working in the neighborhood at the Halifax Infirmary. She could check in on them, when it was needed, and pick them up after her shift finished.

CHAPTER 37

During the mid-eighties the architectural firm developed a solid reputation for meeting design schedules, cost estimates, and minimal change orders, resulting in very happy clients. Dennis was an excellent designer and Lonnie specialized in construction details. Between the two of them the firm prospered and grew in size. Projects were coming in from around the Maritimes based on their reputation to be a good firm to work with. Their projects were recognized and published in design magazines in both Canada and the USA. They received an honorable mention for the golf course clubhouse in Sugarloaf Maine from Architecture USA. The firm was developing a national and international reputation.

The firm grew again and so more design professionals, draftsman, and more support staff were added. Their current office space became too small and the firm had to look for larger space. One project where they had reached the final stages of construction was Metropolitan Place, located by the Holiday Inn just off the MacDonald Bridge on the Dartmouth side of Halifax Harbor. The owners and developers, Jeff and Roger Lancaster, wanted to do more work with the firm and offered a very reasonable rent for Donaldson and Manning Architects. So they decided to relocate the office to Dartmouth. By getting into the building early, not only could they take the entire top floor, they were able to design it to suit the needs of their practice. That decision proved to be of sound reasoning, and improved the proficiency of the firm. So in the spring of 1993 they made the move to 99 Wyse Road, Metropolitan

Place. That floor had excellent views of Halifax Harbor and Halifax itself.

They sold the building on Windsor Street. The closing was June thirtieth, 1993 and with the profits from the sale they were able to purchase a few more Computer Aided Drafting (CAD) packages from AutoCAD, and two more plotters. In addition they paid off the mortgage on the Windsor Street property.

Gone were the older types of drafting machines. Except for Lonnie and Dennis, they kept one in each of their offices, because they were not proficient on AutoCAD like the younger staff. Soon thereafter their staff had increased to four CAD draftsmen, four registered architects, and each one was proficient with AutoCAD.

The new draftsmen were Diane Sloane, David Barton, William Davidson, and Eddie Tasker. The new registered architects were Mitch Thompson, Jon Lavers, Inez Mathers, and John Morrison. Inez was originally from Montréal, Quebec, and spoke and wrote fluently in both French and English—an additional asset.

Since Lonnie and Dennis were in and out of the firm office dealing with ongoing projects, they considered getting mobile phones. Mobile phones were now available but not cheap. Both Lonnie and Dennis purchased one each and were available almost any time for business calls. Kathy was able to reach them with any important calls or problems that needed to be dealt with quickly.

CHAPTER 38

The move to the new offices did not run smoothly. They had planned it for the last weekend in June of 1993. Some of the furniture from the old office was to be moved, but the moving van had brake problems. The moving company then had to send another truck, and move the office furniture from one truck to the other before they could cross the MacDonald Bridge to the new office location. This resulted in the furniture arriving late on the Sunday, and the staff had to spend the first part of Monday getting the office organized. Not insurmountable but a delay in operating. The phones were operating and Kathy was able to take messages for everyone until things settled down.

The firm had taken the entire top floor of the building, the penthouse level. The floor plan was a simple square, with six elevators in the center, and a public lobby with a stair case at either end. The main access to Donaldson and Manning Architects was through a pair of fire-rated glass doors where a receptionist greeted visitors. The waiting area had four black leather chairs with a marble coffee table and several architectural magazines on top. In that reception area, bright artificial lighting displayed many of the firm's important projects on the walls to hopefully impress potential clients.

Pictures of firm projects included Spring Garden Place on Spring Garden Road, a Royal Bank building in Bedford, a four-story office building on the Bedford Highway, several private homes, Knightsridge Townhouses on Trailwood Place in Halifax, Nova Scotia Hospital Mount Hope Center, the

Woodside Ferry Terminal both in Dartmouth, and several schools and apartment buildings around the Maritimes. Those pictures proved that the practice was well-rounded. If they didn't have the proper staff they would find them; if they didn't have the right equipment, they would buy or lease it. It was imperative for them to maintain their high standard of service to clients. That was their bread and butter.

The reception area was the gateway to the board room, located on the northeast corner of the building. It had a commanding view overlooking Halifax Harbour with George's and McNab's Islands in the foreground. There was also a patio outside the board room which was a great place to relax during the warmer weather. Some more prominent pictures of projects executed by the firm were placed on the walls. The north and west walls were of glazed curtain.

The board room table had twelve chairs. This allowed ample seating for architects, clients, and sub consultants for project meetings. There was an overhead projector and two dry erasable boards for conceptual demonstrations. A buffet located along one wall allowed a spot for cups, plates, and sandwiches when required. With the sandwich bar As You Like It on the ground floor of the building, last minute food service was not a problem, when needed.

CHAPTER 39

They also hired three new secretaries. Two of the secretaries were specification writers and the third, Tammy Harris, helped Kathy Wilcox with reception duties when Kathy had other things that needed to be done. Tammy was from Glace Bay in Cape Breton and had a unique way of dealing with people and clients. She was also a crackerjack in terms of finding possible business for the firm. Her computer skills were exceptional and she was constantly checking all major cities in North America for projects requiring architects. She would assemble all the contact information and then have a meeting with Lonnie and Dennis to see if they were interested in the projects.

One day in 1997 Tammy found a design competition advertised for an Embassy in Johannesburg, South Africa, in one of the architectural magazines in the office. Both Lonnie and Dennis were intrigued by this prospect, and then Lonnie remembered a classmate of his who was from Johannesburg. He made a note of the project and having accounted for the difference in time zones he contacted Xander Botsman after he had checked his office information. Xander was pleased to hear from Lonnie and the thought of entering the competition jointly was exciting for him. So they both were in agreement that they would submit a joint proposal for the Embassy competition. Xander mailed the program requirements to Dennis, who retired to his office to study the project requirements in more detail when he received them a week later.

Dennis, after reviewing the project competition documents, had a discussion with Lonnie about a site visit to Johannesburg. It was a necessity in order to fully understand the project requirements and the site in more detail. It was decided that Dennis should make the trip, for he would be in charge of the design for this project if they won the competition. Dennis planned to make this trip a mini vacation and took his wife Sandra along with him.

CHAPTER 40

Lonnie and Dennis had corner offices overlooking Halifax Harbor, Lonnie at the south west and Dennis at the south east corner. Their offices had full-height walls a portion of which were glazed, and with doors for privacy when needed. The registered architects had separate office spaces, with systems office furniture. The rest of the staff worked in an open area at the middle of the office space, divided with system furniture partitions and with tables to allow for spreading out drawings. Each of the occupied spaces had a computer for drawing in AutoCAD, for each of the staff was proficient with that software.

For the flexible office requirements, systems furniture was purchased through Jarvis Marketing of Halifax. Fixed walls were few so space changes could be easily accommodated when staff increased and decreased. Because staff members increased or decreased, depending on workload, the office furniture could be re-designed with ease to accommodate the necessary changes. Robin Jarvis of Jarvis Marketing was available almost 24/7 to organize any furniture changes required by the firm.

A lunch room was located on the northwest corner for staff breaks from work. It had all the necessary items: coffee machine, microwave, fridge, sink, and even a cooktop for staff who stayed through lunch breaks. Like the board room, it had a table and twelve chairs.

Again they were being sought out by developers around the Maritimes. Although some wanted their work done for nothing, Lonnie and Dennis avoided those developers. If a potential client was willing to pay in accordance with the Royal Architectural Institute of Canada (RAIC) fee schedule, Lonnie and Dennis were more than happy to work with them. That led to a strong relationship between the client and the firm.

Staff numbers fluctuated with workloads. Lonnie and Dennis worked with other member firms within the Nova Scotia Architects Association, and staff moved between them to get projects completed. Most firms practiced that kind of staff-sharing. Rather than hiring and firing, a strong workforce could be maintained locally among the different firms, moving back and forth when required.

CHAPTER 41

Lonnie and Patricia looked at where they were living and decided that it was a good time to think of a cottage in a country setting. Patricia liked the south shore and the area around Riverport. So Lonnie, Patricia, and the twins took a few days to travel along the south shore and look for a site that they all liked. The idea was to build a small place to enjoy when they wanted some get-away time. They both wanted to remain members of Ashburn Golf Club, since they had many friends there. The twins were thinking that maybe when their parents were not using the cottage they may use it occasionally.

Lonnie didn't want to be near Indian Path Road; that brought memories of his parents' demise. They liked the area near Lunenburg, and found a nice four-acre lot on Heckman's Island. The lot had an expansive view, looking north into St. Margaret's Bay. The price was reasonable, so they bought it. Lonnie had his old drafting board at home so he began to design a small cottage for all of them. It did not have to be big; just a master bedroom, bathroom with shower, living area, dining and kitchen plus a sleeping loft for the kids when they could join them. The couch in the living area was a hide-a-bed for an additional sleeping area. It was not intended to be a hotel. The deck was oriented due south to take advantage of the sunny days during the summer. Once they had agreed on a design, Lonnie took the sketches to Brad at the office for one of the draftsmen to complete a set of drawings with AutoCAD. Brad had no problem doing a favor for Lonnie; he was still the boss.

The design was simple, wood frame construction, insulated to the National Building Code of Canada standards. The fireplace was in the center of the south wall and on the exterior side was an outdoor fireplace which had its flue parallel to the one inside. The heating system was electric baseboard. While not the most efficient, it was simple and only used when they were there. In the kitchen the cooktop was propane and an additional line was run to the outside location of the bar-b-que. The operating cost was not excessive. During the winter months, all the water lines were drained to prevent freezing. And the exterior windows and doors were covered with sliding barn door coverings and locked for security.

CHAPTER 42

Lonnie and Dennis had several phone conversations with Xander in Johannesburg about the embassy. They had to take into consideration the six hour time difference between Halifax and Johannesburg, so they would call early in the morning to catch Xander at his office in the afternoon.

Dennis and Sandra took the trip to Johannesburg in October of 1998 to meet with Xander and to visit the site intended for the embassy. They flew from Stanfield International Airport in Halifax to New York and then took a direct flight from Newark Liberty International Airport to Tambo International Airport in Johannesburg. Xander and his wife Bella met them at the airport and drove them to their hotel because they were both tired from their long flights.

The next morning after breakfast, Xander and Bella met them in the hotel lobby. Xander took Dennis to the project site and Bella gave Sandra a shopping tour of Johannesburg while the boys carried out their site visit. Bella and Sandra hit it off from the start and enjoyed each other's company. Sandra purchased some colorful scarfs for her girls as gifts from the trip.

The site for the Embassy was on hill with wonderful views north looking over the city of Johannesburg. Dennis took several rolls of film with his 35mm Pentax camera. They would be developed when he returned to Halifax. He also picked up the complete competition package which had topographical maps illustrating the grades and the location of all the services on the site. Next he went to Xander's office to see how the firm and staff operated, and to meet some of the staff assigned to this project.

Dennis and Sandra took some additional time to visit Kruger National Park, with side trips to Pretoria and Cape Town. Since it was October in Canada, it was spring time in South Africa and they were treated to the wonderful blooms of the jacaranda trees along the streets of Pretoria. Next they visited the court house where Nelson Mandela was tried. They both enjoyed South Africa and Dennis looked forward to working on the design competition with Xander.

When they returned to Johannesburg, Xander and Bella met them. They all went to Xander's home and they treated Dennis and Sandra to a meal of South African wild boar, roasted vegetables accompanied by a unique South African salad, followed by a dessert of local fruit, chocolate, and whipped cream. After they had dined Xander drove them back to their hotel and they departed the following morning for the long flights home.

Upon his return to the office Dennis quickly did some sketches of what the building could look like on the chosen site, and sent them to Xander. Xander liked the first cut concepts and then he went to work to complete the conceptual drawings. Between them they put together a very good competition package. It must have been very good because they won the competition hands down. Xander's firm started on the next phase of the project and was constantly on the phone with Dennis. They worked together to get the bid documents together for the project. Dennis and Lonnie learned some things about construction in South Africa since some of the construction materials available were different from those in

Canada. Finally the bid documents were completed and the project went out for bids. Surprise, surprise, it came in under the budgeted amount, a good start. Not only was Xander pleased, but so were the future occupiers of the embassy.

CHAPTER 43

During the early part of 1998 Lonnie and Patricia planned to take the twins away for a skiing holiday during the school March break. Their birthday usually occurred during the time of the break. Since they had introduced skiing to the kids at an early age, mainly at Wentworth Valley, plus Martock Ski Hill near Windsor, they planned a special trip to Sugarloaf Mountain in Maine. Lonnie had a 1992 Volvo station wagon which had more than enough room for them with all their ski gear and luggage. Dennis and Sandra didn't mind looking after Max, their golden Retriever, for that week.

They left on the twins' birthday, Friday, March thirteenth, around eight a.m. and headed to New Brunswick. There were a few wisps of snow on the road but nothing to worry about and the roads were basically clear. The twins enjoyed skiing as much as their parents and were looking forward to Sugarloaf, a ski hill that they had heard a lot about from their friends at Citadel High School.

The road trip was uneventful. They did stop in St. John, New Brunswick at McDonald's for a quick lunch. Since the twins each had their beginner's driver license, after they left St. John, Lonnie let each one of them drive part of the way on the highway between there and St. Stephen, New Brunswick. They crossed into the USA at St. Stephen with no problems. From there they took Route 9 to Bangor, then south on US 95 to US 2 and on to Sugarloaf. They had booked a room with a living room, bathroom, and three bedrooms, one with a double bed and one for each of the twins. They were excited and the conditions looked great. In fact the snow reports for the week looked very promising.

Since it was the twins' birthday Lonnie and Patricia had booked a table at the Golfers Mecca Restaurant for the evening meal as a special treat. It was located in the golf course clubhouse. Lonnie had booked a table that looked up the ski hill and since night skiing was well underway the kids could see a lot of the hill and were excited about skiing the next week. They ordered their meals. While waiting, Lonnie and Patricia had a glass of Pinot Grigio and the kids each had a diet Coke. Since Lonnie and Patricia had skied here before they tried to describe the best runs for the kids. The whole family were accomplished skiers so no lessons were required.

The meals arrived followed by the Golfers Mecca owner and manager. He recognized Lonnie's name on the reservation sheet for the evening and wanted to be there to let him know how successful the restaurant had become and to thank him and his firm for its design. Lonnie remembered him from the first design committee meeting that he and Dennis had in 1981. To show his appreciation for the design of the restaurant their meals were complimentary. Patricia had known Lonnie for a long time and that was the first time she saw him tongue-tied.

The Donaldson family enjoyed a great week of skiing with excellent conditions. They packed up on Saturday, March eighteenth and even though everyone had a good night's sleep, the kids were both dozing most of the way to the Canadian border. The drive was uneventful and all were tired when they arrived home. They unpacked the car and put their things away. Patricia ordered pizza and they put a fire on in the fireplace then they all sat and relaxed after a great week of family fun. They particularly liked the Upper and Lower Narrow Gauge trail. Ben was the only one able to ski it from top to bottom without stopping. Lonnie would get Max on Sunday.

CHAPTER 44

After the embassy project bid period was completed and the construction contract was awarded, construction began a few weeks later. Xander followed the project through construction with very few change orders. The ones that did go through were minimal in terms of cost and design changes. Mainly because Xander's site superintendent worked with the contractor to minimize cost increases to the project and he actually found some construction credits.

Xander kept in touch with Lonnie during the construction phase. There were some specific details that he wanted to be sure were completed per Dennis's design. Due to some of the specific details in the design, additional care had to be taken with the construction to be sure the pieces came together in accordance with the contract documents. Long distance construction advice was not easy. The construction phase for this project was longer than most projects of this size, due to the extra details. The general contractor was adamant that the details be completed correctly the first time.

The official opening was scheduled for October eighteenth, 2002. Both Lonnie and Dennis with Patricia and Sandra traveled to Johannesburg for the event. The twins were twenty years old now. Chloe was attending St. Francis Xavier University in Antigonish and Ben was in his first year at the Dalhousie School of Architecture. Robert and Mary, for simplicity, moved into Lonnie and Patricia's home for the time they were away, to keep Ben company. Ben enjoyed a few games of crib with Robert when his school work was up to date.

The flights were long but worth the effort. Lonnie got to spend some time with his former classmate. Dennis and Sandra headed back to the office where the workload had increased again. Lonnie and Patricia took some additional time after the opening to see some of the highlights of South Africa. Xander gave them some tips on where to go and made some reservations for them. The people, food, and accommodations were all top notch. In particular they both enjoyed the safari in Kruger National Park and the side trip to Cape Town. They also went to Victoria Falls and had a boat trip on the river viewing hippos, elephants, and other wildlife. After they returned to Johannesburg they had a final meal with Xander and Bella who then drove them to the airport to catch their evening flight. They promised to remain in touch with each other.

CHAPTER 45

While the office was expanding yet again, everyone was busy with projects and projects meant cash flow. So on the evening before Canada Day, in 2003, all the staff and their families were invited for an office celebration. Lonnie and Dennis had booked the main dining room at Ashburn Golf Course. Gordie Scott, the new club manager, made all the arrangements for the evening. It was not just a celebration of what Lonnie and Dennis had accomplished, but of what the office as a whole had accomplished together as a team.

Most of the staff was able to attend. Inez Mathers unfortunately had to go back to Montréal because her mother was not well and the family was thinking that perhaps it was time for her to be placed in a senior's home. Inez's father had passed away a few years before and a senior's home would be able to provide her with a comfortable life. The good thing was that her mother was receptive to the idea.

Lonnie arranged for a slide show of all the projects completed since the firm had started. These were going on in the background. Lonnie and Dennis had decided that there would be no speeches, but just impromptu conversations with staff and an opportunity to meet their families. Both Lonnie and Dennis moved separately through the assembled group introducing themselves and having conversations with each of the family members of the employees. Most of the staff's families were not aware of the Johannesburg project and were very interested in the pictures and the country. While the families appreciated the income that they received from the firm, they also appreciated the working environment and camaraderie within the firm.

The sit-down menu included a small bowl of squash soup as a starter, salmon wrapped with prosciutto with a dash of maple syrup, green beans with garlic and roasted slivered almonds, mini potatoes, and pecan pie for desert. Everyone enjoyed the evening and when it came to a close, Lonnie and Dennis stood at the main exit and thanked each one who had attended, and gave each family a bottle of wine from Luckett Vineyards, with a personal label designed by Dennis. Dennis set aside a bottle of wine for Inez when she returned.

CHAPTER 46

Projects continued to flow to the firm. Once again Tammy was researching for potential projects and found several not only locally but also nationally and potentially some internationally. When she had all the documentation in order she sat down with Lonnie and Dennis and they went over her findings. Some led to work for the boards but others, upon further investigation, were not worth pursuing.

At that time, the office was humming along with everyone busy. The mood in the office was a happy one; all the employees enjoyed what they were doing. Well, maybe not all; some staff members, sought work elsewhere. But for the most part, the staff worked together as a team.

There were a few new projects that came to the firm: a P-12 school in Whitney Pier, Cape Breton, a small office building in Bridgetown, a high rise condo project on the Dartmouth waterfront, and a new subdivision of housing off the Kearney Lake Road, along with some low-rise commercial along Larry Uteck Blvd. The development along Larry Uteck grew so fast that the population of that area alone exceeded the town of Truro.

The projects came, were designed, constructed, and completed. Then another project would come along. Not all the years were good. But some were better than others. Sometimes their staff members were borrowed by some other firms as the workload was too low to keep them on, but they were looked after. And occasionally staff were let go because they were not performing up to their potential.

Lonnie and Dennis entered a few more design competitions. They were not always successful, but enjoyed the free thinking part of preparing the concepts. Their method of working on design competitions was simple: conceptual time required would come after the paying jobs were complete, and usually after normal working hours. Sometimes they would stay later than the rest of the staff to review the potential of those projects. The process of running an architectural office was not always a smooth ride.

On a positive note, both Lonnie and Dennis were both nominated for Fellowship in the Royal Architectural Institute of Canada that year. They and their wives went to Toronto for the induction ceremony held in May. Recognition by members of one's profession is quite an honor and they could add FRAIC after their names.

CHAPTER 47

Robert, Lonnie's uncle, had suffered a major heart attack in the fall of 2008 and while in the hospital, passed away a few days later. Lonnie and Margie met to help Mary with the funeral arrangements. Robert was cremated and his ashes were placed in the family plot in Camp Hill Cemetery. The funeral was handled by Snow's Funeral Home on Lacewood Drive. They took care of everything from taking Robert from the family home to the crematorium and then to their parlor on Lacewood for the service. It was attended by Robert and Mary's friends; there were no other immediate family members.

Mary, now in her nineties, was not well, but her spirits were good. Both Lonnie and Margie met with her to decide what was best for her. Staying in the home on Beech Street alone was not possible. The three of them visited the Shannex and The Berkley senior complexes. After much deliberation they agreed on The Berkley on the northwest corner of Gladstone and North Street. Both of Patricia's parents were at The Berkley already so at least Mary had friends close by. Robert invested wisely during his working years and those investments enabled Mary to enjoy her time there without any financial problem.

Both Lonnie and Margie talked to Mary about the time that they spent with her and Robert and how much they appreciated with them both after the death of their parents. Mary commented that both Lonnie and Margie were her children and that she loved them both as if they were her own. Lonnie commented further that Robert was really a father figure for him and that he really appreciated the time spent with him and the introduction to golf at Ashburn. Mary mentioned that Robert enjoyed those times with Lonnie immensely. Mary passed away a few months later and similar arrangements were made with Snow's Funeral Home.

Since they had no children of their own the house on Beech Street was left to Lonnie and Margie to take care of how they saw fit. Margie was now living in Shortts Lake with Robert and their two children, she really had no use for the house. Neither did Lonnie so they agreed that they would sell the home. Lonnie called Sandy to prepare the listing. Because the location was in a popular area of the city it sold within five days with a closing thirty days later. The home inspector's report found that the oil tank needed replacement and so did the electric water heater. These were not great expenditures so Lonnie made arrangements to have them replaced very quickly and the closing went through as scheduled.

Margie planned to use the funds she received to do some upgrades to the landscaping around their home and Lonnie invested his funds with his broker.

CHAPTER 48

During the winter of 2011 the City of Halifax announced a design competition for a Halifax Stadium. The design competition was international. Proposal documents were provided to all firms interested in competing for the project. Since Lonnie was meeting with a client in downtown Halifax when the project was announced, he picked up the design competition package and then took the Halifax-Dartmouth ferry back to the office in Dartmouth. By using the ferry service he saved the high cost of parking downtown alone.

He and Dennis met to review the competition documents. They agreed that the current paying projects took priority over any design competition. Most competitions were a shot in the dark anyway. So they gave senior staff members more authority with current projects, and then Lonnie and Dennis could spend more time on the design competition. Fortunately, the first stage of preliminary concepts was not due for two-and-a-half months. Since they had agreed that this competition would not disrupt any of the current office projects, they planned to remain in the office for a few additional hours each night to review and discuss the conceptual design of the project. Dennis took the lead in design while Lonnie checked possible construction methods. They worked very well together as a team.

The firm spent two months preparing conceptual designs for the competition. Firms from across Canada and a few from the USA had entered this competition. Donaldson and Manning ended up being shortlisted with two other firms, one from Toronto, Ontario and one from Edmonton, Alberta. The final presentations were planned for May twelfth, 2011, at City Hall on Duke Street.

After the presentations at City Hall, the Halifax Council took a few weeks to deliberate over each of the designs. In the end Donaldson and Manning were awarded the project. The main reason, beyond the overall design of the complex, was for the use of solar power to retract the roof when needed, and for the in-floor heating. They also incorporated solar dish collectors for the domestic hot water used in the facility. The solar dishes were manufactured in Amherst, Nova Scotia.

This would be the largest project that the firm had undertaken. Fortunately, local consulting, structural, mechanical, electrical, landscape architects, solar, and interior designers were all identified in the proposal package and accepted by city staff. Each of the sub-consultants was from the Halifax-Dartmouth area and had worked with the firm in the past. Lonnie and Dennis looked at the current projects and juggled the staff so that this project would receive the professional attention that it deserved.

The site selected for the project was east of Highway 118 overlooking Lake Charles near Burnside Industrial Park. The land was currently undeveloped and was easily accessible from the road system in Burnside. Additional roads were being con-structed to improve traffic flow to and from the industrial park. As the land was undeveloped it could accommodate almost any type of design. The stadium was being built for football, soccer, paddling, and archery competitions as well as concerts. Donaldson and Manning, as part of their design submission, had proposed a significant amount of at-grade paved parking, and a parking garage component to accommodate the vehicles required for the seating of twenty thousand spectators and support staff.

CHAPTER 49

When the conceptual design had been approved, the project moved into the next stage, that of preliminary design. In that stage of the project, they endeavored to eliminate potential construction problems, select construction methods, choose appropriate materials, and plan for a smooth construction period. Of course, this phase opened the doors to all the building material supply representatives. They wanted an audience to present their product, hoping that their material or product would be selected, and they could notch another sale. They could be a nuisance, showing up at un-scheduled times. Thanks to the quick thinking of Kathy, the receptionist, she insisted that they schedule an appointment before allowing them into the inner office. Dennis, as the project architect, set aside a morning a week to meet with these product representatives. It usually was a Wednesday morning, depending on his schedule. Sometimes Lonnie would sit in, but with Dennis as the design architect and Lonnie as the architect for the construction, it was not always necessary. Lonnie and Dennis respected each other's knowledge; that made for a successful practice.

Lawson and Logan Architects were not very busy at that specific time, so Dennis and Lonnie arranged to employ some Lawson and Logan draftsman for the stadium project. Both firms had a good working relationship and helped each other out when possible. Lawson and Logan Architects borrowed some of Donaldson and Manning's staff when they were busy with the P3 schools which the province had constructed in 2002.

The preliminary design phase proceeded on schedule. Representatives from the City of Halifax, the Province of Nova Scotia, the Canadian Football League, Soccer Nova Scotia, Paddling Nova Scotia, and Archery Nova Scotia all sat in on that meeting in the company board room. Dennis and Lonnie fielded several questions concerning the design. They noted several minor changes to be made following this meeting. The project was still on schedule. The overall budget was one hundred and fifty million, the largest project the firm had undertaken to date. Funds from Federal and Provincial sources, the City of Halifax, and the Canadian Football League were needed to meet the projected budget. Lonnie scouted out more staff in order to keep the project on track and on schedule.

CHAPTER 50

Lonnie and Dennis had a good working relationship with SunPower, a solar design company located in Burnside Industrial Park. They were all forward thinkers. At the early conceptual design stage for this project, they contacted Sun Power to discuss the possibility of using solar power for the mandated retractable roof. While this had never been tried, SunPower jumped at the opportunity to design and develop a type of solar system that could retract the roof of a large open space. To accomplish this, Sun Power worked with the structural engineers to solve the optimum balance of weight and mechanics for the roof system. The structural engineers, Comeau Engineering, and the electrical and mechanical engineers, M&R Engineering, worked with SunPower from the start to design a roof system where the opening and closing could be powered from energy derived from solar panels. An electrical back up system for the roof system was also part of the design concept.

SunPower was also involved with the solar energy required for the domestic hot water systems and for the in-floor heating systems in the building. The source of water for the heating system was Lake Charles. That water was recycled to the lake at the same temperature that it was when drawn in. The mandate was to prevent any danger to fish or other wildlife in the lake. The solar design required eight separate twelve foot diameter dishes on the south side of the project, unobstructed by buildings and tall trees.

Another use of the sun was of daylighting windows by Advanced Glazing of Sydney, Nova Scotia. While these windows were not vision panels they were of a higher R-value than typical windows and allowed natural light to flood the space. This decreased the amount of artificial lighting needed during daytime use. Lonnie and Dennis had used them on several school projects previously and the results were well received. For this project they were incorporated in the locker rooms, offices, and the Nova Scotia Sport Hall of Fame display center along with other spaces where viewing windows were not a necessity.

EarthNeeds Landscape Architects worked with the natural slopes on the property to develop suitable parking areas, and the best location of the solar power opportunities for the project. The design also took advantage of the minimal slopes to create simple and effective ease of access to the building and parking areas with minimal excavation. Attention was also given to site drainage, with the goal of minimum disruption both to the site and Lake Charles. They worked with SunPower to locate landscaping materials around the solar dishes so that vegetation would not interfere with the function of the dishes. Those dishes tracked the sun during the daylight hours and when the design temperature was reached, each of the dishes would 'go to sleep' and point straight up so as not to overheat the water. These solar dishes were located at the south end of the site and had clear path from east to west to absorb the sun's rays.

The slopes on this site were very manageable for the soil was easy to excavate. Bedrock was, on average, about three meters below the surface, making foundation preparation a relatively simple task. This was unusual in the Halifax-Dartmouth area. The parent material of the soil type was moderately fine-textured, derived from mudstone, shales, and sandstones. Domestic water was not a problem, but sewage was. At least two pumping stations were required to provide a suitable service connection to an existing municipal sewer line. Fortunately, since the City of Halifax had selected the site, they were responsible for providing the services to the site and the City engineers had to design and make the appropriate connections. Electrical and communications services were easily extended from Spider Lake Road to the site.

The site's only access was off Highway 118. Some road construction (not part of the project costs) was designed and put out for bids by the Transportation and Infrastructure Renewal Department. Concern focused on safe entry and exit points to the site. Both roads penetrated the site at two locations. They were five hundred meters each in length, and the overall design had to join up those roads. Dennis ensured that they would.

CHAPTER 51

The area requirements for the stadium were very detailed, and the project requirements were extensive. The area for each program was carefully described, with the detail needed to operate as intended. The four main sports that the stadium would be designed for were football, soccer, paddling, and archery. The football games intended would be a maximum of twelve per year. However, the universities Atlantic Bowl might consider this as a possible location for games in the future. Soccer was scheduled for twenty games per year with, perhaps, an international game.

Paddling was scheduled as much as possible during the spring, summer, and fall months. Banook Canoe Club was in the process of losing its facility to new development and welcomed the opportunity to become part of this major sports project. Paddling would not interfere with any of the other sports and could operate any time when the main playing field was being used. They required a meeting room and storage area for the boats and accessories. At the lake a floating dock was to be constructed with a ramp from the path which led to the stadium.

Archery Nova Scotia was to host a world archery event in 2022 and the Canadian Archery Championships in 2024. There would be other, smaller provincial tournaments along with the National Archery in the Schools Program (NASP), provincials that were scheduled annually. The design also considered that the Royal Nova Scotia International Tattoo may also use the stadium for its annual program.

All the sports had to work together to make their respective schedules work. Each of these sports had requirements for equipment storage, change rooms for competitors, and meeting spaces. Fortunately, the meeting rooms, change rooms, and announcement spaces required were common and could be used by any sport. Equipment storage showed the main difference between sports, and so the space program mandated a separate storage room for each of these sports.

The sports field was to have artificial turf, suitable for football, soccer, and archery. There was a concern that the arrows might damage the sports field, but that was found not to be the case. Any arrows that missed the target skimmed across the surface of the turf. When archery was the event being hosted, a very fine, mesh net was strung across the north end of the field to stop any errant arrows from reaching the seating areas. While there would be no one in those seats during archery events, it was imperative that no damage be done to anything on the north end of the building by an errant arrow.

CHAPTER 52

The space program was developed by the City of Halifax staff prior to the advertisement for the design competition. It had to be detailed in terms of the number of spaces and sizes to meet the needs of all the sports that were to be accommodated in the facility. The overall size of the complex was determined by the size of the football field and the requirement for 20,000 seats plus special client boxes for private seating. Similar to the Metro Center located in downtown Halifax, there were client boxes which were usually pre-purchased by large companies to increase their clients' enjoyment of games.

The Nova Scotia Sports Hall of Fame was going to have a satellite location in the project. The purpose was to highlight all sports that might be active in the stadium, and since parking would be free (actually included in the cost of an event ticket), it provided further opportunity for the ease of patrons to visit the space.

Offices, change rooms, maintenance areas, mechanical areas, storage areas, and washrooms, were located under the slopes of the seating areas. For each of the sports there were special requirements for offices and storage spaces. Fortunately, the meeting spaces could be used by all the sports. The meeting spaces had washrooms nearby and small kitchenettes for the preparation of any food requirements.

The change rooms were specific for each of the four sports to be accommodated. For the football team, each player had a specific locker in the locker room and a washroom with a minimum of four showers. The same requirement existed for the soccer team. During games for each of these sports the opposing team would use the locker for the opposite sport. Both the archery and the paddling sports required male and female washrooms and locker rooms. During major archery or paddling events, the athletes could alternate between these designated spaces. Since a major archery event may have up to three hundred participants, all the locker rooms would be used by the archers.

For maintenance, workstations were located strategically around the building. This allowed the maintenance staff to maintain the building without traveling long distances for the materials required for the specific job. Each maintenance station had mops, buckets, brooms, dust bins, a sink, and the cleaning supplies necessary. There were also closet spaces that included the tools required for regular and minor maintenance of the equipment in the building. If the buildings mechanical system required maintenance repairs beyond the capability of the maintenance staff, an outside specialist company would be brought in to keep the systems operational.

There were two specialty seating boxes: one for dignitaries and another beside it for newscasters, with radio and television crews. The seating in the dignitary box was upgraded for additional comfort.

Archery had a special requirement: a judge's box at field level. This was a temporary structure, which was only used during competitions and was mandated to be designed for easy dismantling and storage.

CHAPTER 53

Michael resurfaced again in Lonnie's life. This time he represented a stadium seating manufacturer. The name of the company he represented was Space Age Seating. He contacted Lonnie and a meeting was set up for Lonnie and Dennis to review the seating products that Michael was representing. Michael was hoping for an exclusive specification from his old friend, since this would be a large contract for him and a significant bonus would result. Lonnie and Dennis treated Michael to a quick lunch of sandwiches from As You Like It along with chocolate squares and coffee for dessert.

The meeting went very well. Although they reached no agreement on the seating products that Michael represented, both Lonnie and Dennis agreed to review the product carefully and to view other sites where the product had been used. While cost was always a major consideration for a project, longevity was also a major concern.

Lonnie and Michael agreed to meet the next day at the Ardmore Grill in Halifax for a quick lunch before Michael departed for Toronto. Michael was at this time living with a lady in Toronto; there was no indication of a permanent relationship as yet. They had a wonderful lunch of deep-fried haddock, with tartar sauce and fresh cut French fries with ketchup, and of course a glass of Coke. They discussed the potential of getting together for a hunting trip back in one of their old haunts near Riverport sometime in the fall.

Lonnie could not wait to show Michael pictures of Patricia, Chloe, and Benjamin. The kids had both grown;

Chloe was enrolled at St. Francis Xavier University, and Ben at Saint Mary's next fall. They were seventeen and had graduated from Citadel High, the new school that had replaced both Queen Elizabeth High and St. Pat's high schools. Michael did not show any interest in Lonnie's children or what school they had attended. He didn't even ask how Patricia was doing.

After lunch, Lonnie drove by the house where he lived with Robert and Mary on Beech Street. Lonnie wanted to show Michael where he lived after his parents' accident. The new owners had kept it pretty much as he remembered, except for a new coat of paint. Again Michael did not show any interest; frankly, he just didn't care. He was only interested in was getting the contract for the stadium seating. Before Michael departed for the airport he mentioned to Lonnie that he hoped Space Age Seating would be given preferred consideration for the stadium project. Lonnie was not sure what to make of his friend from his youth; he was not the same person now.

CHAPTER 54

The stadium was schematically designed from the playing field to the seating since they were the main features. Then the additional spaces were fitted below and around the seating on separate levels as required. The overall plan of the building was that of an oval, to match the playing field. The long portion of the building was oriented north-south and the narrow portion of the building was oriented east-west. For the archery component, shooting north to avoid the sun was the optimum solution.

Structural steel was utilized for the main structural system. Reinforced concrete was used for the foundations, the floors, and the base for the stepped stadium seating. The floors throughout the building were of polished concrete, except for wet areas, like the locker rooms and showers; they were of ceramic tile.

The main entrance to the building was at the south end of the complex. The parking areas were also located there. All patrons had to enter the building at ground-level for purposes of crowd control. The athletes had a separate entrance on the west side of the building. They had a parking lot set aside specifically for their use.

Banook Canoe Club needed space for life jackets, paddles, and canoe storage, and so their entrance was on the east side of the building next to the lake, quite separate from the other sports.

All artificial lighting for the building, inside and out, was from either T8 or LED fixtures. Again, energy efficiency was a prime factor for the building design.

In addition to the main electrical room, there were several electrical closets located around the building so that maintenance staff had ease of access when any electrical problem occurred.

The room areas that required heat had in-floor hot water heating systems and the solar dishes provided the hot water needed. Several areas inside the building had air conditioning, provided by heat pumps. Those were the offices of the staff that were there daily. Fresh air was introduced to the interior spaces through designated systems of ductwork. The sloped seating provided spaces where ductwork could be located. It was not visible and they had easy access when servicing was required, such as the annual duct cleaning.

Interior finishes were primarily painted gypsum board. Door hardware incorporated lever handles and doors were solid core and painted. Some doors required a fire rating depending on the use of the space behind the door. Windows, when required for vision, were triple glazed. That increased the R-value and reduced the overall heat loss from the enclosed spaces. Lonnie and Dennis wanted the building to achieve LEED Platinum status, LEED being the acronym for Leadership in Energy and Environmental Design. That would be a great bonus for the building and for the firm.

CHAPTER 55

The next phase of the project was the preparation of the bid documents. Regular meetings were held with the sub consultants to ensure that they were on track to meet the deadlines required without delay.

Lonnie had a friend, Gordie MacKenzie, one of his regular foursome from Ashburn Golf Course, who was a retired construction supervisor. Lonnie hired him to review the contract documents with the goal of keeping the change orders to a minimum. Change orders always cost more after the fact than if that work had been part of the project. Gordie became part of the design team with his main goal to minimize construction problems and extra costs to the project. His years of experience on large profile projects were very helpful in identifying potential construction issues. He was able to pick up some minor conflicts with the structural drawings and the mechanical drawings which were quickly corrected during the preparation of the bid documents.

The other consultants found that Gordie was easy to work with and they all pitched in to make sure that their part of the project would not cause any construction problems.

All the consultants met the schedule for the completion of the bid package. The structural engineers documents were delayed a day due to a last minute change that Gordie had discovered during his review. Gordie was ninety-nine percent sure that most or all of any construction conflicts were eradicated. At this point all the consultants and Dennis stamped and signed electronically all the bid documents in preparation for the upcoming bid period, which was set at six weeks. The bid documents went via email to Norman Wade Reproduction Services to be printed and held for pickup by interested contractors. Additional sets were sent to the City of Halifax as another location for contractors to pick up bid documents.

Deposits were required for all bid documents taken out by those wishing to bid on the project. Should the documents be returned in good condition, the deposits were given back to that company.

CHAPTER 56

The bid documents were advertised in the Chronicle Herald by the City of Halifax. They were available for pick up on January first, 2013, with bids closing on March fifteenth, 2013. The low bidder would be selected as the contractor for the project. During the first week of the bidding, Gordie noticed a small design conflict between the structure and the sprinkler system design. It was corrected and a design change notice was sent to all the contractors who had picked up contract documents.

Seven large, well-known Canadian contracting firms had picked up the construction documents: four from the Maritimes, one from Ontario, and two from Alberta. Each firm submitted any questions by email to Lonnie since he was the architect in charge of the construction phase. Fortunately, the questions were few since the contract documents were very well prepared.

Several questions per week were sent to Lonnie and he checked with the various consultants to ensure that his response was indeed the correct one. That phase of the project went very smoothly. In the end, the low bidder (and most of the other bids were within a few hundred thousand dollars of the low bidder), was Queen's Contracting. Lonnie reviewed the low bidder's company to be sure that they were competent enough to build this project. The last thing they needed was a contractor that couldn't do the work. Although the firm owners were relatively young in terms of construction experience, they had all come from firms that had built many large and complicated structures around the Maritimes.

The bid documents had clearly stated that the low bidder might not necessarily be awarded the project if any problems could be found with their past work. After careful review, it was decided to award the project contract to Queen's Contracting in the amount of $98,783,567. Queen's Contracting offices were located in Burnside Industrial Park close to the project site.

At that time Lonnie was in Cape Breton carrying out inspections on another project, so Dennis attended the ceremony on behalf of the firm. Dennis met all the members of the City Council along with some of the funding partners for the project. Each expressed their satisfaction with the design and the fact that the low bid was within the project budget.

The award ceremony was held at City Hall on a Friday afternoon, followed by seafood appetizers and wine. Queen's Contracting along with all their approved sub-contractors were invited and in attendance.

Michael was in attendance on behalf of Space Age Seating as their bid was the low bid received for the project. Michael was ecstatic, cheerful, and perhaps had a little too much wine as his speech was becoming slurred and a little too loud with his Lunenburg accent. Dennis escorted him out of City Hall to the Barrington Inn across the street and made sure he got to his room safely, and then returned to the celebrations. After the award celebrations, Dennis called Lonnie to tell him about Michael and how he had behaved inappropriately at the award ceremony. Lonnie was concerned for not only his partner but also his childhood friend, what was happening to him.

CHAPTER 57

Sometime after the award celebrations, Dennis was hearing that Space Age Seating was experiencing problems in some other stadium projects. The quality was not consistent with the shop drawings provided at the time of tender. Apparently, over time, when the seats were used frequently, the steel frame that held the fiberglass seat and back failed. The reason that the steel frames failed was they were a thinner profile than the shop drawings submitted for approval prior to the bid period. That fact alone had caused several seats to collapse in some other stadium projects.

Lonnie and Dennis discussed this issue and booked a few days away from the office to personally review the concerns. Lonnie called Brenda to get them to the airport and they flew in Lonnie's plane to Toronto and then to Winnipeg. The prime purpose was to view the problems of the seating on other projects for themselves. They found that the Space Age Seating support system as installed in both the Toronto and Winnipeg stadiums was indeed not consistent with the shop drawings that had been submitted for approval of the seating for the Halifax Stadium. Further, Space Age Seating had not issued any notice of these changes prior to bidding on the project since the shop drawings issued were those of the original manufacturer for the support system. So, legally, the shop drawings that were approved at time of tender by Space Age Seating, and the product intended for use, were fraudulent.

After what they found, they had no choice but to issue a change order to break the contract for the Space Age Seating.

Michael was furious and called Lonnie. "You broke the contract!" he shouted. When Lonnie tried to explain the faults his firm had found in Toronto and Winnipeg, Michael kept shouting, "You goddamn son of a bitch, I thought we were friends, you broke the contract!" and hung up. That was disturbing personally to Lonnie, but the decision had been made; Space Age Seating was removed from this project as a sub-contractor.

Queen's Contracting began discussions with Olympic Seating, the next low bidder for the stadium seating. The end result was that Olympic Seating agreed to supply their seating for the same price that Space Age Seating tendered, so there was no change in the overall contract price; that was a blessing in disguise. Olympic Seating had been used on several previous stadium projects to date and with no failures or problems.

CHAPTER 58

In the first phase of the construction, they cleared the site of any trees that were within twenty feet of the building location. This was followed by the excavation sub-contractor, whose job was to prepare the site for foundations, parking areas, and services. Mardo Construction, a local firm, was the sub-contractor for Queen's Contracting; they had considerable experience in and around Halifax, Chester, and the Valley. They made short work of the necessary site work with three excavators, two dozers, and enough dump trucks to move the suitable material around the site. No material had to be trucked off-site, since the design was based on the principle of zero earth removal. The first thing they did was to prepare an area for the construction trailers, site office, and washrooms. For the twenty-four-month construction phase, this would be home for all the contractors. Most had their own construction trailer or made arrangements with other sub-contractors to use theirs. The general contractor's trailer had a room with a table and chairs for project meetings.

Power was brought into the site from Spider Lake Road, at the north end, so that the line avoided going over or under Highway 118. The overhead lines stopped at a pole on the site and then went underground from there to the temporary panel for all the sub-contractors' use during the construction phase. That temporary panel was the future site of the transformer and pad needed for the complex. Then all power was installed underground to the building's main electrical room. Most of the contractors had hand tools that were battery operated, which eliminated most of the typical power cords running around a construction site.

The area for the stadium was cleared quickly of trees and excavation was started for the foundations. Almost all the trees suitable for lumber were stripped of branches and then trucked to Elmsdale Lumber for preparation into construction lumber. Elmsdale Lumber was pleased to get these trees at a reasonable price and Queen's Contracting was just happy to have them off-site. The remaining branches were run through a chipper truck and saved for future landscaping. A win-win for both.

Honey Huts provided the temporary toilets, and several were located around the site. Their pumper truck visited the site each week to remove the waste and replace the required fresh supplies.

Backhoes were used for excavating the building foundations and the dozers prepared the parking areas and the base for the parking garage. Once an area had been excavated and was not to be disturbed again, the landscaping contractor got an early start on his part of his contract. At the north portion of the site, since no further work was required there, he could do the minimal landscaping in accordance with the contract documents.

Where the at-grade parking areas were located, they were cleared, graded, and compacted to the grade required for the gravel layer. The details required a twelve-inch compacted gravel base before the two-and-a-half-inch base coat of asphalt was laid. This became a clean area for the storage required for the project and greatly reduced the amount of dirt and mud that would be tracked around the site.

CHAPTER 59

Unbeknownst to Lonnie and Dennis, Space Age Seating had called their lawyers shortly after their contract was canceled with the intent to file a lawsuit against Donaldson and Manning Architects and Queen's Contracting. After much internal discussion in the offices of Space Age Seating, the lawsuit was filed in the Nova Scotia Supreme Court on Monday May twelfth, 2014. Donaldson and Manning and Queen's Contracting were served on Friday May sixteenth, 2014 by a process server at their offices. The lawyers for Space Age Seating were Murphy and Greene, a high-profile law firm in Toronto, with branches across the country. The Halifax branch of Murphy and Greene was located in Purdy's Wharf Tower Two.

Lonnie and Dennis retired to the board room to discuss the situation and asked Kathy to call their lawyer, Tom Broady. Tom was not in; he had gone to Chester to play a game of golf with some old school friends. But Lonnie had his cell number and Tom answered on the third ring. Tom had just started the second hole, a par three that ran parallel to the ocean when he took the call, knowing that if someone called his cell, it was important. He walked and talked alongside his battery-operated power caddy on the way to the next green. After hearing the grounds for the lawsuit, he advised Lonnie and Dennis not to worry at this point because there were lots of things to do in preparation for the case. The first thing he would do on Monday morning would be to contact Murphy and Greene for more particulars and then he would meet with Lonnie and Dennis later that afternoon.

Kathy came into the board room after the phone call and poured two glasses of Chivas Regal scotch, one for Lonnie and one for Dennis, for she knew that they were both upset. Lonnie advised Kathy to pour one for her and to join them. She had been with Lonnie and Dennis almost since the partnership was formed, and was a major part of the team. They all discussed the reasoning behind their decision to issue the change order to cancel the Space Age Seating contract and all agreed that it was the appropriate thing to do given their findings from their recent trip to Toronto and Winnipeg.

While Kathy had both of them together she went over a few office items that needed their personal attention. That did not take too much time as they were cleared up very quickly. The conversation returned to the lawsuit.

Lonnie and Dennis did not get much sleep over that weekend.

CHAPTER 60

On Monday, May nineteenth, cement trucks arrived to begin pouring the footings for the building. Cement pumper trucks were used to get fresh cement to the required locations. After the footings had cured for five days, the walls or columns were formed for the next pour. These steps were followed rigorously because the foundation contractor, Built Rite, worked to complete their part of the contract as scheduled. Queen's Contracting worked well with the project sub-contractors but were very strict with the timelines. After all, it was important for them to complete the project as per the schedule. In addition, there was a bonus for finishing on time or earlier for all the trades depending on how they met the schedule.

Structural steel that had been fabricated by RKO Steel Limited began to arrive on site. It was stored in the same area that previously had received the base coat of asphalt on the west side. All the steel had been prime-painted before it had been trucked to the site. The erection cranes, from A.W. Leil Cranes and Equipment, were positioned in such a way that they would not have to move after they were set up. They carefully unloaded the steel components from RKO, and placed them in specific numbered locations to ease the erection phase, when it was scheduled.

Shaw Pre-Cast Solutions of Lantz had cast the stepped sections for the stadium seating. They also started to arrive on site and were placed in the same area prepared for the storage of large construction items. There were also some pre-cast columns for the project, and they also began to arrive on site. Each piece was numbered and placed in a manner that would allow for ease of erection when the time came. All the parts of the project were like a jigsaw puzzle, their placement was specific, or otherwise the project would not come together as planned.

Oversized overhead doors in the complex allowed the larger pieces of construction equipment to move freely around the interior of the complex both during construction and after completion.

CHAPTER 61

Lonnie and Dennis met with their lawyer, Tom Broady, the following Monday afternoon. Tom said that while he understood that both of them were concerned about the lawsuit, only one member of the firm was really necessary to get up to speed on the case and to follow through with all the necessary requirements. So Lonnie took the lead and Dennis went back to the office, for the other projects in the design stage on the boards needed his attention. Lonnie and Tom spent the rest of that afternoon going over the options in the case.

Tom called the Architects Liability Insurance (ALI) firm, located in Toronto, and informed them of the lawsuit. Since Lonnie sat in the board room of Broady Clarkson, the call was on the speaker phone. ALI questioned Tom as to how he planned to prepare for the case and advised that they would be sending one of their lawyers to Halifax to assist. Tom would take the lead because he was more familiar with the project, the people involved, and the prime basis for the lawsuit.

The reason Space Age filed the lawsuit was the loss of income due to the canceling of their contract. Their contract was cancelled by the general contractor, Queen's Contracting, after Donaldson and Manning issued a change order stating that the Space Age Seating product was no longer acceptable. The issue before the Courts would be, was this change order a breach of contract?

Tom pointed out that there would be an exchange of phone calls and letters and relevant documents before it proceeded to the next step. Then the parties would be "discovered," a legal term for being orally examined by each of the opposing lawyers, with a court reporter recording the questions and answers. After that, a written transcript would be produced by the court reporter.

Murphy and Greene made several motions before the Courts seeking all documents, the drawings, change orders, and specifications which pertained to the decision to cancel the contract with Space Age Seating. A list of witnesses for each side was produced and forwarded to each of the parties involved. Murphy and Greene were not in a rush to get to court; they wanted to review all the construction documents, letters, and emails before they began the discovery process.

CHAPTER 62

The structural steel for the roof was complicated. The rails for the movable portions of the roof had to be perfectly level to allow the solar powered batteries supplying the electric motors to function when needed to open and close the roof. If the sun was not cooperating, the electrical backup system would be utilized. Each section of the roof had to overlap at the joint of the next movable panel so that rainwater could be directed to the roof drainage system. And each roof section was arched to allow water to flow to the exterior rainwater collection channels of the roof system. The center of the roof was the highest point and the slopes were, from the center, north, south, east, and west. Half of the roof moved to the north end and the other half moved to the south end of the stadium. This of course made for some complicated overlapping of joints when the roof was closed, but that was required to ensure that rainwater would not leak to the playing surface below. Dennis followed the structural engineers design process very carefully as he did not want the required structural design to impede the overall visual appearance of the roof component both externally and internally.

The weight of the overall roof system, since it was movable, required additional structural support with beams and columns that were hidden within the exterior walls of the stadium. The solar panels were designed to energize the storage batteries that would provide enough power to open and close the roof when weather permitted. The backup system to open and close the roof was electrical. Maintenance staff would be directed to ensure that no rain was in the forecast before the roof was opened. There were several meetings on the roof system between the architects, Sun Power, M & E Engineering, and Comeau Engineering to ensure that all the possible issues were professionally considered prior to the final design of the roof system. This would be the first stadium project to utilize a solar system for opening and closing the roof.

Dennis took the lead in these meetings since he was determined that all the consultants understood the importance of getting the solar operated roof system correctly installed. Sun Power was concerned that the weight of the roof may impede the intended operation. Comeau Engineering stressed that the operation of the roof system should work as intended since each of the roof parts were carefully designed as balanced in weight components. Each section of the roof would weigh the same as the next and that the resting place for all the roof sections, when the roof was open, was designed to support its total weight. M&E Engineering confirmed that the electrical design included enough power to open and close the roof when the sun was not cooperating.

The exterior skin of the building was designed to be bold and colorful, so insulated aluminum panels were used. The colors selected were based on the Nova Scotia flag: white, blue, gold, and red. Below those panels were insulated precast concrete panels, also cast by Shaw Pre-Cast Solutions of Lantz.

When there was a game or other activity in the stadium, the artificial lighting was designed to be integral with the building's precast concrete columns, with the light directed to the playing field and spilling over the spectators from behind them. This system provided a seemingly natural lighting quality for the sports field and the seating areas.

Part of the project program was the sound system and it was designed to allow all areas of the seating to hear the words of announcers and game plays at a sound level as consistent as possible with normal conversation. This design eliminated high pitched or low sound enabling all spectators to hear the process of the activity clearly, without echoes or other sound disturbances during any of the sports being played or performances.

With the exterior of the building close to completion, the mechanical and electrical contractors could begin their interior work. A large electrical conduit ran from the transformer pad to the stadium main electrical room. From there, like the tentacles of an octopus, an enclosed conduit ran to several of the sub panels in the building. Each sub panel was dedicated to a specific area of the building. Black and MacDonald were the mechanical and electrical contractors for the building. Robert Thomas was the foreman for Black and MacDonald on this project, and he made sure that all his workers performed well and that there was the appropriate cooperation between the mechanical and electrical divisions.

Sometimes on construction projects, should one sub-trade not be able to get to the job on schedule, the other sub-trade might not respect that component, and just do their part of the contract. Then problems would occur after the fact, resulting in arguments between the trades involved and then delays would occur.

CHAPTER 63

With the ductwork now in place and the electrical work all roughed in, the wallboard installers moved in. Steel studs were placed, then the drywall was installed. The subcontractor for this trade was Pinaud Drywall and Acoustical, another local company located in Burnside close to the building site. They were so proficient with the stud, drywall, and joint taping installations that call backs were minimal. All studding was secured to the floor with PL premium adhesive because the floor could not be penetrated with mechanical fasteners due to the fact that it had in-floor heating cables installed. Since this was the main project that they had contract for currently, Pinaud Drywell were able to devote a high percentage of their labor force to the stadium project and completed their contract ahead of schedule, something that rarely happened in the construction business.

After the drywall was installed, taped, and filled, the painters moved in. Lovett Painting Services was the subcontractor for painting the project. Most of the walls were spray painted, and extreme care was taken not to get paint on the polished concrete floor. Drop cloths were placed wherever they painted. The colors that Dennis chose were light colored earth tones because the games being played were, in fact, outdoor games.

Next, the hard tile was installed in the locker rooms floors, walls, and shower areas. The color of the tile was again in the earth tone range, selected by Dennis, to match the color palette that he had chosen for the overall project. The size of the tile was a half meter square with tight joints to eliminate the need for wide grout lines that would eventually get dirty over time. All the countertops in the locker rooms and throughout the building were granite supplied by Nova Tile and Marble, located in Burnside. The granite was installed at the same time as the other finishes. The overall appearance of all the finishes was neutral.

Then the interior doors, frames, and hardware were installed. All the doors were pre-painted before installation and Lovett Painting Services touched them up where needed after installation. Lever-handled door handles with a stainless steel finish were used throughout the building. All exterior entrance doors were glazed. The overhead doors that were required for the Banook Canoe Club boat storage area, which faced the lake, were installed at this time.

The entire building was handicap accessible, and all doors were a minimum of a meter in width to accommodate wheelchairs. Within the stadium, seating on each of the levels was identified for handicap spectators. The elevators in the complex were designed with accessibility in mind and so were each of the levels of the building. Each of the four elevator banks had strategically placed areas for wheelchair patrons. All washrooms were also handicapped accessible. Furthermore, there were no steps on the exterior of the building since all entrances were ramped up slightly to meet all the entrance doors.

The interior and exterior light fixtures were installed next. All the fixtures incorporated LED or T8 lamps, depending on the specific location in the building. For the sports field, Vingreum 300 watt LED floodlights were used. These same fixtures were installed on the exterior of the building just below the aluminum panels and also installed in the parking garage and the at-grade parking areas. They were aimed downward to prevent any issues with aircraft heading to Stanfield International Airport. These fixtures provided the daylight appearance that Lonnie and Dennis envisioned for the project when they were originally preparing their design submission.

CHAPTER 64

Four containers arrived on site with the stadium seating from Olympic Seating based in Mississauga, Ontario. Each seat was individually wrapped in recyclable material and easily transported to its final position. From there they were assembled in place. The steel frames were bolted to the pre-cast concrete risers. They were also bolted to the next seat frame in that row, for additional structural support. Each seat was then numbered and lettered in accordance with the contract drawings and specifications. Olympic Seating had an on-site representative to ensure that the seating met or exceeded the approved shop drawings. Lonnie reviewed the approval documents with the on-site representative from Olympic Seating.

One of the last sub-contractors on the site was Sports Fields of Sudbury, Ontario. They were the supplier and installer of the artificial grass for the sports field. Due to the anticipated use of this sports field, it was decided to go with synthetic turf as it could be played on twenty-four hours a day, seven days a week. This part of the project was left to the last since the sports field area was a great place to store all other the products that would be installed in the rest of the building. The specifications for the sports field included a twelve-inch gravel/sand sub-base with drains on the sidelines, turf of nylon fibers attached to a porous polyethylene backing, two-inch infill of crumb rubber placed within the fibers, and a polyethylene pad just under the backing for extra cushioning.

Now that the project was nearing completion, the final layer of parking material could be completed. Since Nova Scotia does have problems with frost during the winter, extra care had to be taken with the base material. Prior to the first and second layers of asphalt being applied, all base material was fully compacted. The parking areas were graded to allow all storm water a natural path of return to the lake.

The landscape contractor came back on site to complete his work. The overall plan was to reduce maintenance on a continual basis, in order to lower operating costs. The design included low shrubs and ground covers with a few trees to keep maintenance to a minimum. There were no lawns to fertilize, water, or mow anywhere on the site. Not only did this cut down on maintenance, but it also decreased the requirement for landscaping tools and a dedicated space to store them.

Lonnie was in Cape Breton doing the final inspection for a P-9 school in Glace Bay. Regardless of the lawsuit, the site inspections for the other current projects had to be completed and finalized prior to their contractors receiving final payment. For the stadium project, all the sub-consultants were on site to inspect their specific part of the project for errors or omissions from the contract documents. Deficiency lists were prepared by each of the sub consultants and by Donaldson and Manning. Dennis, in Lonnie's absence, assembled the final list of deficiencies. Most were minor except for one section of the office area. There was a report stating that all the fans were operating as intended. However, this was not correct, since the electrical inspection found that one of the ventilation fans in the office area had actually not been wired. The inspector for the ventilation system was verbally chastised and discharged from M&R Engineering. Apparently that inspector made the mistake of assuming that the work was complete since the other fans he had inspected were done correctly, so he didn't check them all. Assumptions do not work in the construction process. The wiring for the fan was now completed, as specified.

Each of the sub consultants prepared their specific list of deficiencies and Dennis compiled them into a complete list of items found that needed to be corrected. Because of the continual inspection by all the sub consultants throughout the duration of the project, the final deficiency list was minimal. Each of the consultant's final deficiency lists was forwarded to Donaldson and Manning and they compiled the full list for Queen's Contracting. To expedite the process, the design team sub consultants emailed their list to the respective sub-contractors. All the sub-contractors and Queen's Contracting worked to complete the correction of the deficiencies.

The purpose of these inspections was to ensure that the project was completed in accordance with the approved construction documents. Donaldson and Manning were adamant that each of their clients received the product that they had paid for and were very diligent with their inspection reports.

CHAPTER 65

Since the project was now completed, on Saturday, August twentieth, 2016 the City of Halifax hosted a concert of local maritime musicians and bands to celebrate. Sarah McLachlan, originally from Halifax, now living in British Columbia, was one of the star attractions. Others included Natalie MacMaster, Dave Gunning, Heather Rankin, and The Rankin Family.

The ceremony opened with Mayor Michael Savage cutting a ribbon at center field. Lonnie and Dennis were given the honor of holding the wide blue, gold, red, and white ribbon, colors symbolic of Nova Scotia's flag, for the cutting ceremony. They were piped into center field by the Nova Scotia Highlanders Pipes and Drums band. The Lieutenant Governor of Nova Scotia was also there, dressed in his official uniform. He was on center field with members of the City Council, the wardens of each county, and with the local Member of Parliament, Andy Filmore.

After Mayor Savage cut the ribbon, a twenty-one-gun salute signaled the opening of the stadium. Then the dignitaries along with Lonnie and Dennis and families retired to the spectators' box located next to the news booth on the upper floor overlooking center field. There they were served drinks and seafood appetizers.

Lonnie and Dennis were constantly observing how the dignitaries and the general public interacted during all parts of the opening ceremonies. They were both nervous and concerned that the building may not perform as they had intended. They carefully watched how the patrons entered the building and went to their assigned seats. Was the signage adequate? Did the patrons appear confused while searching for their assigned seat? Were the handicapped individuals able to access their assigned seat without any difficulty? From their observations there appeared to be no standout issues as the persons attending appeared to find their seats with relative ease. The ushers remained in their assigned positions and interacted with the patrons periodically.

The stands were filled to capacity with people from all over the province. Seats were assigned on a first come, first serve basis and for no charge. The seats were allotted on a percentage basis, depending on the population in each of the eighteen counties of Nova Scotia. Each county had a specific area assigned for seating. That allowed all Nova Scotians an equal opportunity to see the new stadium that a portion of their tax dollars supported. In order to get a seat for the opening ceremony all Nova Scotians were given ample notice to go online to the City of Halifax website, Halifax Stadium page and follow the steps to secure a seat or seats, seven days prior to the opening.

It was a lovely day in August and the roof was opened. After the opening ceremonies, the various musicians played several songs to the delight of the audience. When the sun faded in the west, and darkness arrived, fireworks were set off from a Banook Canoe Club raft in the middle of Lake Charles and were clearly visible from every seat in the stadium.

After the ceremonies had finished, the audience started to leave. Since the exit stairs and the elevators were placed in prime locations, above the National Building Code require-ments, the patrons could easily depart in an orderly fashion.

The elevators worked efficiently and those that took the stairs had no problem in exiting the building in a safe manner. That was one of the true tests of the building's functions. Those leaving the parking garage and the parking lots had no problem departing the site via the exit road. Lonnie and Dennis were extremely pleased that the building performed as designed, from the initial conceptual drawings to the final completion of the construction. They breathed a sigh of relief and both experienced an overall satisfaction with what they had been able to achieve with this project.

CHAPTER 66

The warranty period began August first, 2016, and covered one year from that established completion date. While perhaps this was not enough time for all construction problems to develop after completion, it was the industry standard. Certain products had warranties that extended well beyond the project warranty period. These included some of the following items: stadium seating, lighting fixtures, plumbing fixtures, door hardware, solar collectors, and of course the retractable roof.

The stadium maintenance personnel could contact Lonnie about deficiencies when they arose. Then Lonnie would contact the general contractor who in turn would contact the responsible sub-contractor about the deficiency. While perhaps not the most direct route, a paper trail was mandatory to ensure that all items received the attention that they deserved and were corrected or replaced in a timely manner. Contract wise, it was the general contractor who was ultimately responsible for the project deficiencies.

Lonnie was in contact with the general contractor weekly to review the status of the deficiencies. Sometimes because the sub-contractors were off on other projects it was difficult to get them back to complete their work on deficiencies. However, since final payment was held back until their portion of the contract was completed, that was the impetus for them to complete their work in accordance with the contract documents. It was not long before all the items of deficiency were corrected and final payment was issued to the general contractor. They in turn paid out the sub-contractors.

The basis of the lawsuit weighed heavily on both Lonnie and Dennis. This was supposed to be a time of celebration since the firm had just completed their largest project to date, and retirement for both of them was not that far off. Succession planning was on their minds. Who could or would take over the firm? But that could not even be considered any further until the lawsuit was resolved.

After the opening of the stadium, Tom Broady called and requested Lonnie's attendance at several meetings to review the case. Friday of the following week, August twenty-sixth, 2016, was set aside to review the first details of the lawsuit. The firm had the necessary liability insurance mandatory for the practice of architecture; nonetheless, all aspects of this case had to be carefully examined. Tom reviewed the pros and cons of the lawsuit. The legal firm for Space Age Seating was Murphy and Greene of Toronto, and the case was being handled by their satellite office in Halifax.

Tom went over the motions that were before the courts and the list of witnesses for the case. All the pertinent information requested by Murphy and Greene had been forwarded to their local office. Tom had met his obligations in regards to the request for documents about the decision to change the supplier of the seating.

Since the trial was not scheduled until December, Tom told Lonnie to try and relax, for he had a strong feeling that the case might be cancelled before it actually got to the courts. Tom thought that perhaps Space Age Seating might just drop the case. While Lonnie liked that idea, he was not convinced, knowing how stubborn Michael could be.

CHAPTER 67

Following the completion of the stadium, the firm was constantly busy with several other projects. There were a few small office buildings both in Truro and Sydney, Nova Scotia. They also were working on a high school in Fredericton, New Brunswick and a new large animal building for the veterinary college in Prince Edward Island. Dennis was busy with the conceptual design of a small Sportsplex in Saskatoon, Saskatchewan. There was some necessary site information missing from the documents he had received from the town, and Dennis wanted to walk the site one more time in case he had missed anything the first time around.

Lonnie had pre-booked a limo ride to the airport with Brenda. Lonnie and Dennis took Lonnie's plane and were gone for a few days leaving Brad McPhee, the more experienced architect in the office, in charge along with Kathy, who would call Lonnie or Dennis in the case of an emergency.

The flight was a long one with several stops for fuel along the way, but Lonnie and Dennis had an opportunity to discuss the future direction for the firm. Lonnie graduated forty-four years before in 1971 and Dennis graduated from the School of Architecture at the University of Manitoba in 1975. Both were thinking of retirement. Perhaps Lonnie would before Dennis, but the transfer of ownership was on both their minds. They had developed a good working relationship with respect for each other, and they had a very good partnership agreement, so no major problems were anticipated.

After landing in Saskatoon, they rented a car and drove to the site. Dennis wanted to walk around and get a feel for the land and the surrounding area for a second time. The project property bordered on a wildlife preserve, and Dennis thought that perhaps a raised viewing station should be incorporated in the building for people to view the animals in the preserve, especially the buffalo.

After the site visit, they went downtown to the offices of Recreation Saskatoon to meet with the planning committee. The meeting went well and the committee was enthusiastic about the concept of the viewing station and approved it on the spot adding it to the space program. After some coffee and sandwiches, Lonnie and Dennis left the building and drove to the Best Western Hotel near the airport. They checked into the hotel and then went for a swim in the indoor/outdoor pool, talked, and just relaxed. That evening they ate in the hotel and talked more about the transition of the office partnership. While no concrete decision was made, it stayed on their minds for future discussion.

The following morning they each had a breakfast of orange juice, eggs benedict on whole wheat toast, and a few cups of coffee. Next they collected their suitcases and briefcases, checked out, and headed to the airport for the long flight home. Lonnie called Brenda to see if she would be available to pick them up when they returned. Her response depended on the time, but that it should not be a problem. She asked Lonnie to call again about ninety minutes before arrival.

CHAPTER 68

On the flight home, Dennis mentioned that he was experiencing some health issues and that he had booked an appointment with his doctor for the following week. Dennis's medical appointment came and went, but several other appointments involved specialists. Over time Lonnie noticed a difference in Dennis. He was pale and tired most of the time. Still a determined individual, he put his time in at the office like anyone else. His wife Sandra was concerned and talked to Patricia about his condition.

The final results were not good; Dennis had lymphoma, a cancer of the lymphatic system, part of the body's germ-fighting network. The prognosis was bad. Lonnie and Dennis met in the boardroom the morning after he had received the news, and they gave each other a strong hug. Although at one time they had wanted to cancel their partnership insurance with Bell and Grant Insurance, they were happy now that they had it because it was very useful for this exact situation. Sandra would be able to continue to live the life she had with the kids and would not have to move from their home. Lonnie advised Dennis, saying, "It is time for you to leave the office and spend the time you have left with your family. We will get your projects completed, as you intended. We've got your back." Dennis replied that he would come in periodically to check on projects when he was feeling up to it.

Lonnie and Dennis called their senior architect, Brad McPhee, into the boardroom to explain the changes that were forthcoming. Brad would now take the lead on several of

Dennis's projects. Dennis would be available on-call as much as possible. Brad had known something was up, but he was shocked at the news from the senior partners.

CHAPTER 69

In the court case, Murphy and Greene requested three days for discovery and both parties agreed upon September twelfth to the fourteenth. They were to meet in Murphy and Greene's Halifax office. It was agreed by both parties that the discovery examination is held without order by the consent of the solicitors. It was further agreed that the discovery transcript may be used at trial or subsequent proceedings in accordance with the rules pertaining to discovery examination and the rules of evidence without the necessity of calling the reporter in formal proof of the discovery examination.

Lonnie had cleared his calendar for those dates. He wanted to be in attendance when each one was being discovered for this case. The witness list for Space Age Seating included Michael Whynott, Art Wilson the installer, Kenneth Cole the president of Space Age Seating, and Mark Ryan the manager of the Vancouver Stadium. Witnesses for Donaldson and Manning were Lonnie Donaldson, Gordie MacKenzie, Jack Usher from the Winnipeg stadium, and Hans Myer from the Toronto Stadium.

During the discovery period, Verbatim Inc. of Dartmouth, Nova Scotia attended each session and recorded every word said and provided a written record for the courts. Each of those present for the discovery were questioned by the opposing lawyer. The records of the discovery would be made available to all parties involved through their respective legal representative following the completion.

So that all the witnesses could be finished with discovery by September fourteenth as scheduled, the discovery went until seven p.m. on the last evening. The witnesses for Space Age Seating left and headed to the Five Fishermen restaurant on the corner of Carmichael and Argyle Streets for a late evening meal. Lonnie and Dennis took their witnesses and Stephen Cooke of ALI to The Upper Deck on Lower Water Street. The transcripts from the discovery followed four weeks later in mid-October.

The trial was set for December fifth to the thirteenth of 2016 and the courts had set aside nine full days to hear both sides of the argument.

CHAPTER 70

Work in the office continued as usual, although there was a cloud of concern by the staff. However, they picked up the pace since Lonnie and Dennis were not in the office as much now because of the court case and Dennis's health problems. Brad had no problems filling the positions required for each of the projects on the boards at that time. John Morrison was also a great help. When John visited construction sites he kept his ears open and was able to bring a few new jobs to the firm. The staff members were strong supporters of both Lonnie and Dennis at this time. It was after all their firm.

The firm had entered a design competition for the waterfront in Québec City. Dennis, even though he was only in part-time, provided much of the design concepts for the competition. Inez Mathers, a junior architect, was completely bi-lingual and she made sure that all the competition documents were written in French. The other members of the firm rallied around Dennis to make sure that the competition documents were completed for delivery to Québec City on the day scheduled for submission. There was a delay in receiving the final drawings from the printing company. So in order to make the deadline, Lonnie and Inez flew to Québec City in his plane and hand delivered the competition package to the Québec City Town Hall on the day they were due.

The firm was successful in winning that competition, so Inez took the lead for the project and was in constant contact with Dennis, sometimes by phone or FaceTime when he was not in the office. The follow-up submissions went in accordance with the schedule as set by Québec City.

The firm was busy with other work in and around the Maritimes. Projects on the boards at that time were a school in Labrador City, a small municipal office building in Mabou, Cape Breton, a housing project in Yarmouth, Nova Scotia and a golf course clubhouse in Fredericton, New Brunswick. The staff worked together like a well-oiled team and the production of the projects went very smoothly.

While the firm had CAD printers in the office, now most of the projects had their respective contract documents sent electronically to Norman Wade Reproduction Services for the printing of the contract documents for local projects. If reproduction services were available in the location of the projects, the documents were sent there electronically for reproduction. Gone were the days of calling the drawings "blueprints;" now they were known as "whiteprints." The drawings and documents were printed and assembled and each respective client or designated representative became responsible for issuing them to the contractors interested in bidding for the work. A deposit was required for each set of documents issued, as a means to cover the cost should they not be returned.

The lawsuit weighed heavily on Lonnie and Dennis. Both were losing sleep. They knew that canceling the contract with Space Age Seating was the right thing to do professionally and the friendship with Michael had nothing to do with that decision. Their decision was based purely on the knowledge of the problems being experienced with the revised seating support system found in the Toronto and Winnipeg stadiums.

CHAPTER 71

The trial began on Monday, December fifth in the Supreme Court of Nova Scotia in Halifax on Lower Water Street between Donaldson and Manning Architects and Space Age Seating. The lead solicitor from Murphy and Greene, Gabriel Greene, began to present his client's case to judge Harold Matheson, for there was no jury at this trial. The reason for the lawsuit was the loss of income by Space Age Seating, from a 2.48 million dollar contract for the stadium seating. Their star witness was Michael Whynott, Lonnie's childhood friend. Lonnie was doubtful that they could remain friends after the trial. For sure, future hunting and fishing trips would be canceled.

Michael, when called to the stand as a witness, elaborated how hard he had worked to get Space Age Seating specified for the stadium project. He listed the number of trips he had made to Nova Scotia from Toronto for visits to the architect's office with catalogues and samples of materials all of which cost his company time and money. Gabriel examined Michael all morning and, after a break for lunch, until two ten p.m. Then Tom began cross examination.

Lonnie noticed that Michael seemed quite confident when being questioned by Gabriel; his rehearsed answers flowed flawlessly.

Tom cross-examined Michael on the steel supports for the seating in Toronto and Winnipeg and why they were changed from the approved shop drawings on those projects. Michael replied that the change in the steel support system had no effect in the overall seating supports. Tom questioned Michael further about issues with Space Age Seating at the Toronto stadium and the Winnipeg stadium. Michael stated that he was not aware of any problems with the seating at those two stadiums. Tom was getting nowhere with Michael, although Michael did look nervous. Since Tom was getting nothing from Michael about problems with the seating as installed at other stadiums, he finished with Michael at four fifteen p.m.

However, when Tom cross examined Michael, Lonnie observed that he was on guard and even appeared to be on edge. No matter how hard Tom tried, he could not get Michael to admit that he was aware of the problems with the change in the steel support system.

Lonnie was thinking that Michael's testimony in regards to the trips, catalogues etc., was true but he failed to mention that the steel support supplier was changed from what was submitted on the shop drawings. Lonnie noted that Michael was fidgeting nervously in his seat. Lonnie couldn't sense any of the confidence Michael displayed when they had first met to discuss the stadium seating. To Lonnie, Michael appeared to be hiding something.

Tuesday morning Gabriel called his next witness, Art Wilson, whose company had been contracted to install the seating. Gabriel began his examination of Art at nine fifteen a.m. and went to eleven forty-five a.m. at which time there was a break for lunch. During his testimony Art mentioned that this project would have been the largest project that his company had undertaken to date, and the loss of income was substantial. Judge Matheson seemed to be swayed by Art with his loss of income due to the cancelation of the Space Age

Seating contract. Judge Matheson made several notes during Art's testimony. The court finished in the morning at eleven fifty a.m. and resumed at one p.m. Tom's cross examination of Art finished at two forty-five p.m. Tom saw no benefit to examine Art any further since there was nothing to be gained from it. When he finished with Art the court retired for the day.

During Art's testimony Lonnie felt sorry for him and his loss of income that his company would have earned for this project. However, the issue for Lonnie was the quality of the items being installed and Space Age Seating's change of supplier for the structural supports was the main reason for issuing the change order that canceled their contract. Lonnie was not sure what to think of Art's testimony. Judge Matheson appeared to be very interested and he took in all that Art had said while he was on the stand. Lonnie was concerned that the judge was more concerned about Art's loss of income than the issue of the seating not being stable.

On Wednesday morning Gabriel called Mark Ryan, manager of the Vancouver Stadium. Gabriel questioned Mark on the quality of the Space Age Seating. Mark responded that he was having no issues with any of the seating in terms of the steel frame supports. Tom made a note to do some checking that evening on that installation, as he was intrigued by Ryan's response to questioning in discovery.

Tom also noted that Gordie left the courtroom early that afternoon. Gordie did some research on the stadium seating in Vancouver and learned how that seating support system had been manufactured by the original supplier and was of good quality. Next, he discovered that Space Age had contracted with a different manufacturer for the seating steel support system to reduce their overall costs of their product. That new manufacturer used a thinner profile of metal for the support system. That was the main cause of the current problems in the Winnipeg and Toronto stadiums. That was not properly documented when they originally bid on the Halifax stadium project. The shop drawings provided during the bidding period were of the original steel supports and did not reflect the change to the thinner profile. Gordie reported his findings to Tom that evening.

Thursday morning, Gabriel called the president of Space Age Seating to the stand, and he continued in the same vein; the loss of considerable income due to the cancellation. Tom had the opportunity to cross examine each witness. He did not spend much time on each because his star witness was Lonnie. What he did note, with the exception of the Vancouver Stadium, was that the witnesses avoided mentioning that Space Age Seating's product was not only having problems with the steel frame seating supports, but also former clients were having trouble with the stated warranty of the product. They were not getting corrections made in a timely fashion. These were just a few of the things that Lonnie and Dennis discovered prior to issuing a change order for the stadium seating contract. That day the court adjourned at four fifteen p.m.

Lonnie noted that Judge Matheson paid considerable attention to the president of Space Age Seating. He discussed the effort that they put into getting the job and that the cancellation meant they would have to lay off staff since they had very little work on at this time. At this point Tom questioned the president of Space Age Seating in regards to the change of the steel structural supports for the seating. The president just shrugged and said as far as he knew the supports for the seating worked just fine.

On Friday morning, Gabriel had the opportunity to re-examine his client on the items Tom had raised with his client, and that lasted for about forty-five minutes. Tom did not follow up with additional cross examination. Space Age Seating had finished with their witnesses and now it was Tom's turn to call his witnesses on behalf of Donaldson and Manning, which followed after a short break.

Lonnie was wondering how this was going to end up; he was not feeling comfortable about this trial. In particular he did not like what he observed with the trial judge.

CHAPTER 72

Before the trial started Tom met with Lonnie to review some of the questions he was going to ask and to prep him for some of the questions that Gabriel may ask him. Tom made sure that Lonnie would be comfortable with some of his questions and they reviewed some of the answers together. He told Lonnie to answer each question as truthfully as he could as he didn't want him to be tripped up during the trial. He did prepare him for some of the types of questions that Gabriel would ask as it was Gabriel's job to try and discredit Lonnie for his actions in regards to the seating.

The first witness Tom called was Lonnie, who was sworn in after taking his seat in the witness box. Tom wanted to spend a lot of time questioning him, for Lonnie was his star witness. He questioned Lonnie on the original decision that he made regarding the stadium seating. Lonnie described how Michael, a personal friend at the time, had talked to him on several occasions about Space Age Seating. Michael had brought samples of the product seating material, and catalogues describing and illustrating the seating with connection details. Lonnie was forthright with his answers, short and to the point as directed by Tom prior to the trial. He went on to say that when the specifications were being prepared, there was no indication of any problems with Space Age Seating, and following their research they were one of the seating systems that were specified for the project. The Space Age Seating bid was carried by the successful bidder, Queen's contracting.

It was not until he found out at a later date, after the construction contract was let, that some stadiums were having problems with the Space Age Seating. That after their investigation was completed they issued the change order to reject the Space Age Seating supplier. Lonnie and Dennis had visited Toronto and Winnipeg stadiums where they learned of serious faults with Space Age Seating. Because of that trip, both he and Dennis decided to issue the change order for that portion of the contract. That was the only reason for the change order issued to Queen's Contracting for the stadium seating.

Lonnie was looking directly at Judge Matheson during his period of questioning; to him it appeared as if the judge was half asleep.

Tom asked Lonnie to explain the problem with the seating that led to the issuing of the change order, resulting in the canceling of the contract, and if there were other issues to be considered. Lonnie stated the main reason was the issue with the steel framing. He also mentioned the delay of the non-existent repairs to date on other stadiums projects, after numerous complaints from previous installations which he and Dennis discovered on their trip to the stadiums in both Toronto and Winnipeg.

Gabriel wanted to spend time with Lonnie on cross examination. He knew he could not gain anything positive, but he did try to trip him up with a few questions. One question Gabriel asked was, "Do you have a home theater in your home"?

Lonnie replied, "Yes."

Gabriel then asked, "Who is the manufacturer of that seating you used?"

Lonnie replied, "Space Age Seating."

Gabriel then asked, "Do you have any problems with that seating?"

To which Lonnie replied, "No."

Then Gabriel asked, "Then why would you cancel the contract of Space Age Seating for the stadium project?"

Lonnie replied very quickly, "Because the steel support system was changed from the seating I had purchased for my home to a product of lessor quality and there was significant evidence that failures were becoming commonplace with that product in the stadiums we visited." Lonnie went on to say that Space Age Seating issued fraudulent shop drawings in regards to the actual product they had been intending to install and that they had installed in two other stadium projects, namely Toronto and Winnipeg.

Gabriel moved away from those questions very quickly and started another tack. In fact some of his next questions were downright insulting, given Lonnie's experience in the industry. Gabriel asked Lonnie why he took so long to get registered after graduation from university. When Lonnie tried to explain that he wanted some experience in municipal planning prior to seeking the required experience in architecture, Gabriel cut him off quickly. Next he questioned Lonnie on his delay in going to university after high school. Judge Matheson seemed quite attentive during this line of questioning. Finally Tom interjected and approached the bench and requested that Gabriel cease this line of questioning as it had nothing to do with the trial. Reluctantly Judge Matheson agreed with Tom and requested that Gabriel move on. Gabriel responded with, "Nothing further, your honor."

Judge Matheson noted that Lonnie had Space Age Seating in his home but seemed to be thinking of something else during the remaining line of questioning; he certainly did not appear to be making any notes or taking in the full testimony of Lonnie.

On Monday morning Tom called Gordie MacKenzie to the stand to discuss construction problems with the stadium seating. Gordie mentioned that the problems with Space Age Seating were caught in time to issue the change order for the stadium seating. Tom asked if Gordie was aware of the problems with Space Age Seating and Gordie replied that he was aware firsthand of the problems. He said he had recently attended a Blue Jays game in Toronto and just happened to sit in a Space Age seat that was broken. With that statement Tom and Lonnie both noticed Gabriel feverishly making notes. At the same time they both noticed that Judge Matheson appeared to be thinking of something else.

When Tom had finished with Gordie, he called Hans Myer, manager of the Toronto Stadium. Tom asked Hans his opinion of the Space Age seating in the Toronto stadium. Hans said that he was disappointment at the delays in his attempts to get the Space Age Seating repaired. He went on to say that now there were many seats that were unusable; the stadium could not sell those seats for their scheduled events and they suffered a loss of income. Tom asked Hans how many times he had contacted Space Age Seating for the necessary repairs, to which Hans replied, "To date we have had four phone conversations, we have sent three letters, the last letter was registered and from our lawyer. So far we have not had an indication as to when the seats will be repaired." Gabriel did not spend much time with this witness; he knew there was nothing further to gain.

Lonnie was again observing Judge Matheson who appeared to be daydreaming throughout this line of questioning and nothing seemed to register with him. Lonnie was concerned since it was important for the judge to understand why the change order that deleted Space Age Seating's bid was issued in the first place.

Next, Tom called Jack Usher, the manager from the Winnipeg Stadium. Jack stated the same things that Hans had mentioned. Tom went over each of the questions he had asked Hans to reconfirm the problems that both stadiums had experienced with the Space Age Seating. Gabriel again chose not to cross examine; he had nothing to gain by doing so.

After closing arguments from both sides, the trial ended at two thirty p.m. on Tuesday, December thirteenth. Now they had to wait patiently for the judge's ruling.

CHAPTER 73

On March sixteenth, 2017, Judge Harold Matheson ripped the tendering system because the seating for the new stadium was not awarded to the lowest bidder. He stated that the architects were not acting in the best interest of the Province or the City of Halifax by canceling the Space Age Seating contract. He said that they had provided no proof at trial that the Space Age seating was not of good quality. He disregarded the architect's findings from previous stadium projects that had installed Space Age Seating. Judge Matheson said that the testimony given by Lonnie Donaldson was weak and inconsistent, and revealed a person having doubtful knowledge and limited experience. He went on to say that every taxpayer would agree that this level of waste in projects of this nature is unacceptable. He further wrote, "Great oaks of waste grow from little acorns of unnecessary expenditure." Lastly he stated further, "The change order was not warranted."

Gabriel Greene said that this ruling marked the first time a supplier had successfully sued over the awarding of a contract. Judge Matheson awarded Space Age Seating one hundred thousand dollars in losses and ordered Donaldson and Manning's liability insurer to cover the legal expenses of Space Age Seating. Tom, Stephen, and Lonnie met the day after the decision to discuss what went wrong at the trial. Tom suggested that it was best to wait a few weeks until things settled down. The Chronicle-Herald printed the decision on the front page of the Friday, March seventh issue. That was a black mark against Donaldson and Manning Architects. Former clients called Lonnie to express their concerns since they were extremely happy with both the firm and the quality of the work that they had received. Current clients expressed dismay at the decision, because previous work that the firm completed for them had no problems. They suggested that perhaps the decision was flawed.

Lonnie took a few days off from the office, leaving Brad in charge. Wentworth was only an hour and thirty minutes away, so he took Ben and Chloe up for a few days of skiing to clear his head and to spend a few days with them. They stayed at a friend's chalet, and it was a good time to reconnect for they were twenty-five now. Chloe was teaching at Halifax West High School and engaged to a lawyer that she had met a few years ago and she had an in-service day that Friday. Ben was working in his father's firm, as a junior architect. Lonnie had to get permission from Brad to take Ben out of the office for Friday, but it was good father-son and father-daughter time.

CHAPTER 74

After a few weeks of time to settle down, Lonnie met again with Tom to review any options. Tom was pissed; this case did not deserve that decision based on the facts presented at trial. As far as Tom was concerned, the judge erred in his decision. They agreed to file an appeal, and this was encouraged by the Architect's Liability Insurer (ALI).

The appeal was filed on April tenth, 2017. The prime reason for the grounds of the appeal were that judge Matheson erred in his findings that:

The findings of the architects from other projects of installed Space Age Seating were flawed

The Space Age Seating contract should not have been canceled based on the issue with the steel supports

The architects erred in their decision to cancel the Space Age Seating contract

There was no difference in the steel seat support system

The appeal could not be heard until October 2017. The courts were backlogged with many cases currently and Tom could not expedite the process of the courts. Lonnie and Dennis were furious but there was nothing that they or Tom could do to speed up the process.

Work in the firm continued. Some new projects currently on the boards in the office included a P-8 school in Musquodoboit Harbour, a four-story office building in Kentville, and a twenty-three-story condo project in downtown Halifax. Outside the province, there was a P-12 school in

Cornerbrook, and a new park building for Gros Morne National Park, Newfoundland. The other projects that the office was working on were in the construction phase and the site superintendent was kept very busy with inspections.

The method that Lonnie and Dennis had adopted for taking a project from beginning to completion followed the Royal Architectural Institute of Canada (RAIC) manuals with some small personal variations to suit their practice. This method was followed by everyone in the firm.

Lonnie and Dennis also assisted graduate architects that were hired by the firm with their requirements for professional practice, assistance for which each was grateful.

Dennis was not doing very well and was spending most of his time at home now. When he was able he communicated via Skype.

CHAPTER 75

As December approached both Lonnie and Tom had met several times in November to go over the process for the appeal. The dates set aside for the appeal to be heard were December twelfth and thirteenth. Tom was fully prepared and rehearsed his presentation with Lonnie.

The day of the appeal arrived and Tom's opening statement to the appellate court's three judges was simple: the courts shouldn't be in the business of second-guessing architects' decisions. He went on to argue that the architects were concerned that the issue with the steel support system on the Space Age Seating put spectators at risk of injury. The prime reason for making the change in contract to Olympic Seating was client safety. He argued further that the specifications were very clear, that where the materials are not provided in accordance with the specifications, that does not lock the architects into awarding to the low bidder. He went on to say that Space Age Seating did not disclose the fact that they made a change to the steel supports as the shop drawings provided at the time of bidding did not reveal the revised support system. In fact, he stated that their bid was actually fraudulent as proper documentation was not provided. After all, client safety is paramount for any project.

The architects spent time researching the products for seating and although a change was made, it was made in good faith for a better product for the overall good of the stadium. Tom also pointed out that the construction specifications of the contract documents were very clear on that point. He went on to state that it's a thoughtful process; it's not like a trip to Kmart.

Gabriel attempted to refute all of Tom's arguments but made a negative impact on each of the appellant court judges.

Justice Sterns noted that in Division 01-General Requirements, the contract documents state, "Should problems be found with any specified product and not corrected to the satisfaction of the architect that change orders may be issued on that product." Justice Jones said, "Based on those findings of the courts, architects would be in court every time a supplier disagreed with a decision."

Justices Sterns, Harrison, and Jones of the Nova Scotia Court of Appeal reserved decision. While the courts had allowed two days for the appeal, only one was required.

CHAPTER 76

Work continued on projects in the office. Lonnie was not in the mood for many questions, so the staff did their best to stay out of his way until the results of the appeal were known. Brad became the "go-to" person for questions regarding the projects that were in various stages of the standard architectural process in the firm.

Some new projects in Nova Scotia, currently on the boards in the office included a P-12 school in Amherst, a six-story office building in Bridgewater, and another multi-story condo project off Dunbrack Street in Halifax. Outside the province, there was a P-9 school in Edmundston, New Brunswick, and a new park building for Brackley Beach, Prince Edward Island. The other projects that the office was working on were in the construction phase and the site superintendents were kept very busy with inspections.

The method that Lonnie and Dennis had adopted for taking a project from beginning to completion followed the Royal Architectural Institute of Canada (RAIC) manuals with some small personal variations to suit their practice. This method was followed by everyone in the firm.

Lonnie, and Dennis when he could, also assisted graduate architects that were hired by the firm with their requirements for professional practice, assistance for which each was grateful.

The findings of the appellate court came down eight weeks later and were very clear. The appellate court justices were unanimous in their decision: "The architects are the ones that make decisions on building products, not the supplier, and the change order was warranted." They went on to say, "The evidence discloses that Space Age Seating's unilateral deviation from the shop drawings in other installations would lead to a reasonable inference that they would do the same thing at the Halifax Stadium." And they stated further that "the learned trial judge had no juridical basis for that finding." Because the decision of Justice Matheson was overturned on every issue, all costs were awarded to Donaldson and Manning. ALI was so impressed with the manner in which Tom had worked with them on the case that they agreed to contact him if other court cases arose in the Maritimes involving architects' liability.

The results of the appeal were not important enough to be on the front page of the Chronicle-Herald the next day; they were buried on page seventeen between the Walmart ads for shirts and underwear.

Lonnie and Dennis were ecstatic and called everyone from the office into the large boardroom to inform them of the court's decision. It was a time for celebration. Since it was late on Friday afternoon, Kathy ordered sandwiches, soft drinks, and sweets from the As you Like it lunch counter. She also ordered a few cases of Dirty Blonde from Nine Locks Brewery on Waverley Road. Everyone breathed a sigh of relief and talk could then turn to the current projects on the boards and CAD screens. It was a perfect end to the week and a very long and exhausting court case.

CHAPTER 77

As Dennis's health deteriorated, his calls and visits to the office decreased. Lonnie took some time to visit him and Sandra whenever he could. It was sad for him to see his friend and partner fading away. Dennis enjoyed the visits and discussed the practice, the growth, and the success of the firm.

He passed away on March twenty-eighth, 2018, shortly after the appeal results were announced. Lonnie and Patricia assisted Sandra with the funeral arrangements. The celebration of life and the service were held in Snow's Funeral Home on Lacewood Drive in Clayton Park. Lonnie was asked by Sandra to say a few words during the service.

Lonnie was not really comfortable with public speaking especially in regards to his friend and partner, but in this case he rose to the occasion. He described how he had met Dennis at a meeting of the NSAA and how that meeting had developed into a very successful partnership. Lonnie stated that the partnership was not without some heated discussions on some projects but those discussions resulted in good projects and happy clients. He mentioned some of Dennis's more notable design projects, like the golf course clubhouse in Sugarloaf in Maine, USA, the embassy in Johannesburg, South Africa, and the recent completion of the stadium project in Dartmouth. He went on to say that Dennis's approach to design was to listen carefully to the client's needs and then to use the chosen site to make the client's wishes become a reality with the design of the building. That had resulted in many happy clients and had created a very successful practice. He closed by saying that he would miss his friend and partner and he passed on condolences to Sandra and her daughters.

Dennis was cremated and his ashes were placed in an urn that Sandra kept on a bookshelf in the study, as she was not sure where she wanted to have them interned for the moment. Dennis was originally from Manitoba and his family had a burial plot in Winnipeg so that was a possible final resting place. Sandra would deal with that matter at a later date. Sandra held a small reception following the funeral at the family home on Brackley Place in Clayton Park for close friends and family. She knew that she would have to find ways to remain busy. Their girls, Barbara and Shirley, were in their early thirties now, both married and with families of their own. Sandra would be busy with the grandkids, and that would occupy some of her time. Patricia made sure that Sandra became part of her foursome at Ashburn, especially on Tuesday, the girls' nine-and-dine nights.

The workload for the firm seemed to increase again.

CHAPTER 78

Lonnie Donaldson was again working late at the office. It was early fall 2019 and this project was due to go out for bids the following week. The client, Transportation and Infrastructure Renewal Department (TIRD) wanted to maintain the schedule they had set for the project, a new P - 9 School for Middle Musquodoboit, and keep the local member of the Nova Scotia Legislative Assembly happy. Coordinating the pre-bid documents was not an exciting job for an architect, but paramount to a successful project.

The rest of the staff had left for the evening and Lonnie was alone. Occasionally he would look out from his seventeenth floor office located on the penthouse level of Metropolitan Place, Dartmouth. The view across the harbor to Halifax was impressive and he enjoyed watching the cruise ships when in season. Two docked at Pier 21 at that moment. He dreamed of a time he and Patricia could take a few cruises someday.

Patricia, Chloe, Ben, and Barbara were probably enjoying a final round of golf at Old Ashburn and then a fine meal on the deck overlooking the eighteenth hole. If he was lucky, there might be some leftovers when he arrived home later in the evening, so he decided not to order out. However, for occasions like this he opened the bottom drawer of his desk and took out a bottle of Glenlivet Scotch and a Montecristo No.4. Knowing that the air handling system would remove the cigar smoke from the office by morning, before the staff arrived, he snipped the end of the cigar and lit it. He enjoyed watching the smoke rise to the ceiling as he exhaled. Then he poured three fingers of scotch, and sipped slowly as he watched the lights coming on in the buildings across the water. In the harbor the ferry service was operating as usual, both ferries leaving their respective docks of Halifax and Dartmouth in unison and passing in the middle of the harbor.

All of a sudden he heard "Lonnie, are you smoking those damn cigars again?" It was Betty, one of the offices cleaning staff. "Oh, hi Betty, the air handling system will take care of it before morning," he replied. "Yeah, but it still stinks while I am working here," was her retort. Then she said, "I will come back later, got other floors to do before I finish up tonight."

As Betty departed, he glanced back to the drawings, and looking at drawing 704 he noted that the electrical engineer had specified a pot light housing which would extend fourteen inches above the finished ceiling. Unfortunately, this was in conflict with the structural drawings which had a concrete beam located in the same position. Lonnie made a note to inform the electrical engineer that a revision would be required. He added this to the list of other conflicts and items that needed to be dealt with before finalizing the construction documents. The fewer change orders on a project, the better.

Around nine p.m. Lonnie decided that enough was enough and it was time to head home for the night, the rest could wait until the morning. The cigar smoke smell was almost gone by now. Lonnie packed his briefcase, and then just decided to leave it where it was until morning. Since he was walking towards the front entry to get his coat from the closet, he began thinking that retirement was not that far off. He and Patricia could do without the burden of working every day. But until that day arrived, there were still several projects to be completed and hopefully he could sell the firm to some of the senior shareholders.

He put his coat on and after setting the security alarm behind him, he headed to the elevator. While walking to his car, he thought he heard someone call his name. So he turned toward the voice, a voice which sounded all too familiar. Next he heard, "Lonnie, you son of a bitch!" then two gunshots. It felt like someone punched him hard in the chest and after putting his right hand there; it felt wet and he had a nauseated feeling. Then a third shot rang out. As he lay on the cold concrete slab, he thought he heard sirens in the distance. He struggled to maintain consciousness.

CHAPTER 79

Lonnie woke up from his coma-like state forty-six hours later, in a bed at the Halifax Infirmary on Summer Street. Patricia was asleep by his side; she stirred when he moved and groaned. She immediately called for the duty nurse who called the doctor on duty and she answered very quickly. After the doctor checked his vital signs, she turned to Patricia and gave a thumbs up. She mentioned to Patricia that the stiches would have to be removed within seven to ten days and that their family doctor could perform that service. The doctors and staff at the hospital were top notch and responded immediately for every part of Lonnie's recovery.

Patricia gave a sigh of relief and a few tears appeared in her eyes. The twins were downstairs in the hospital cafeteria, but reacted very quickly to Patricia's text and rushed upstairs to their dad's room. Patricia was crying a silent but happy cry. Ben and Chloe were also crying over the fact that their father was alive and well. The twins were trying to both hug him at the same time. It was a happy family moment.

Lonnie was still a bit confused about what had happened. Detective Rennehan of the Halifax Police force was outside the room at this time and pleased that Lonnie was recovering. Lonnie questioned him as to what had happened that night he was shot and who was the culprit. Detective Rennehan said first that it was Michael Whynott that shot him. He added that from what could be determined by the Halifax Police Department, Michael had lost control of his senses and blamed Lonnie for his loss of income on the stadium project seating.

The police department had investigated Michael's latest movements since he left Toronto a few days before the shooting. They had found that he became estranged from his family, ditched his girlfriend, and lost his job with Space Age Seating. He sought revenge and made a suicide pact with himself. Since his life, in his opinion, was no longer worth living, he was going to take Lonnie with him. He was an excellent shot with his .38-caliber revolver, having practiced often at the shooting range in downtown Toronto. That was evident from the two shots that hit Lonnie on the left side of his chest.

Lonnie asked about the third shot he heard. Detective Rennehan hesitated, but said that Michael had committed suicide. The detective added that he found a note in Michael's pocket that detailed the reasoning behind the attempted murder. Michael was convinced that Lonnie wanted nothing further to do with him and he saw himself as a complete failure. Michael had been observed lurking around Metropolitan Place for a few days waiting for Lonnie and the opportune moment to carry out his revenge for canceling the Space Age Seating contract.

Lonnie was saddened to hear that bit of news. After his recovery he planned to reach out to Michael's mother. Michael's father Arthur had passed away previously, but Carla was still alive and living in a smaller house across the river in Pentz. Lonnie asked Patricia to call Carla, to pass on his condolences and to promise that he would be down to visit as soon as he was able.

The reason Lonnie survived was that unbeknownst to anyone, he had a condition called *Dextrocardia situs inversus totalis*; his heart was located on the right side of his chest. Although sometimes associated with other medical problems, Lonnie's condition had no effect on his overall health. In fact this condition actually saved his life. If his heart had been in the normal position, Patricia would be planning a funeral instead of a homecoming celebration.

His doctor discovered on the internet through Google that this condition affects an estimated one out of every twelve thousand people and that gender, race, and ethnicity do not seem to have any impact on whether or not a person develops this condition. While some people with this condition may have other health issues, in Lonnie's case there were none; he was otherwise in perfect health.

Patricia was dumfounded; she had known Lonnie for a long time and never suspected that he had any kind of issue like that which was being described to her at the moment. Nonetheless she was very happy that he had this condition, for he was still alive.

CHAPTER 80

Lonnie's recovery was slow but steady, and he now had time to think of what he wanted to do in the future. Ever since Dennis had passed away, Lonnie had been increasingly thinking about retiring.

Patricia was scheduled to retire from nursing in a few weeks and was hoping that Lonnie would retire soon. She was playing more golf now, at least four days a week with her friends.

Lonnie's thinking was interrupted by Brad MacPhee who had come to visit, to see how he was doing and to update him on current firm projects. Brad mentioned that the firm was still compiling all the ongoing necessary documentation to meet the LEED requirements for the stadium project.

The opportunity was there, so Lonnie asked Brad what he thought of taking over the firm. Brad was surprised because he had not expected Lonnie to consider retiring. He said that he would certainly think about that option. Current project schedules were put aside (they were in good shape anyway) and Brad and Lonnie discussed the ways and means of how Brad could take over the firm. Lonnie suggested that perhaps Mitch and Inez might join him in a new partnership. Brad thought about that and about the number of projects that were currently underway in the firm.

Lonnie and Brad discussed the sale of the firm in great detail. The number of projects on the boards in the office at this time was a great asset. Brad mentioned that he would like to have Lonnie provide some guidance for at least a year following his retirement.

After an hour or so, Brad thought he should leave and give Lonnie some time to rest and himself some time to think about becoming an owner of the firm—a very successful firm. When Brad left, the food service cart brought Lonnie his evening meal: meatloaf, lukewarm mashed potatoes, peas, water, and Jell-O for dessert. Lonnie could not wait to get home to a good home-cooked meal!

The following morning, Lonnie's doctor came in to report that all his vital signs were good, and that he was ready for discharge. The doctor advised that he would need time to recover at home for at least three weeks before returning to the office. Lonnie called Patricia, and she came to the hospital quickly to help get him get ready for home. She brought some clean clothes for him to change into from the hospital Johnny shirt. Staff insisted that he take a wheelchair to the exit.

Patricia had gone to the parking lot, paid the fee, and drove to the front door to pick him up for the trip home. His stay in the hospital had given him time to think about what he could do with his life after retirement. Woodworking was an excellent way to pass time, along with golf, travel, trips south in the winter, and both hunting and fishing. Perhaps a fishing trip to Newfoundland, up the west coast to River of Ponds might be in order. All those seemed promising from his hospital bed and now he had a few weeks to consider these options in more detail. It was time to let the younger generation take over the firm.

CHAPTER 81

Lonnie recovered quickly and followed the stipulated few weeks of rest; he was back in the office working on projects again. Brad had moved into Dennis's former office, and so Lonnie went there to discuss the current status of the projects. He also wanted to discuss his retirement. Brad understood Lonnie's desire to retire, and was prepared for this conversation. Although perhaps not the proper time to discuss the financial side yet, Brad was willing to buy the firm. He mentioned to Lonnie that he had discussed it with Mitch and Inez, and broached the possibility of the three of them buying the firm. Mitch was not interested because he was planning a move to Montréal since his wife, a heart surgeon, had just accepted a position as head surgeon at the Montréal General Hospital. They were both from Montréal originally and were looking forward to returning. However, John Morrison, a much younger member of the firm, was very interested in a partnership.

Brad said he would arrange a meeting with all of them to discuss the matter further. There was no rush yet, but when Lonnie wanted something to happen, and had made up his mind, then things usually happened quickly, and Brad was fully aware of Lonnie's situation.

They met the following week to discuss this prospect further. The value of the firm was based on the "work in progress" at the time of sale and the resulting profit from those projects. Brad and Inez, after a price was established, were able to purchase outright. John was not in a position to come up with his entire share on the established purchase date. Lonnie spoke to John separately, and suggested that perhaps he could make a down payment for his share and then pay off over time without interest. John was very pleased with that proposal, and very eager to become a shareholder in a firm that had such a good reputation.

Patricia was happy that Lonnie would be retiring soon. The twins were set in their lives. Chloe was happy as a teacher and recently trained as a Basic Archer Instructor (BAI) for the National Archery in the Schools Program (NASP) at Halifax West High School. Ben was working on his license to practice and membership with the Nova Scotia Association of Architects, and said he would keep his father posted on the progress of the firm.

Lonnie and Patricia played more golf and spent more time at the Heckman's Island cottage. Occasionally they would invite Beverly to join them with her new man, Bill Martin, also a member of Ashburn, not a good golfer but he had potential.

Epilogue

After all the paperwork had been signed off in the spring of 2019, and most of the money from the sale of the firm was safely with his investment manager, Lonnie started to relax a bit. While he still was obliged to go into the office periodically for the next twelve months, to advise the new owners of dos and don'ts, he was no longer attached to the decisions that the firm made on a day to day basis. He was sleeping better, and he and Patricia enjoyed getaways to the cottage any day of the week now. They always texted the twins whenever they went down to Heckman's Island.

From their home they had a wonderful view of the North West Arm, and the Royal Nova Scotia Yacht Squadron. It had a southern exposure to take advantage of the sun. Thinking ahead they had built their home primarily on one level for their retirement years.

Ben was doing well with the firm and was looking forward to becoming a junior partner. Lonnie would help with the cost when the time came. Ben was also involved with a structural engineer who also did work for the firm, Barbara Lohnes. She had graduated from Dalhousie University, and was employed with Comeau Engineering. Interesting was the fact that Ben had met her at Ashburn Golf Course when they were both junior members. They had been living together for four years. Lonnie and Patricia both liked Barbara and she was welcome addition into the family. Marriage was something that might occur down the road but not a concern. Times had changed!

Chloe's husband was originally from Vernon, British Columbia, and was a lawyer with Broady Clarkson in Dartmouth. They had met several years before when Lonnie had helped Chloe with a legal problem that happened when she had a small car accident on her way to work one day. Her lawyer for that case was Rory Woods and a relationship developed over the dealings with that case. They were married on August eighteenth, 2006, and had their first child, Ryan on May eighth, 2011.

Occasionally Lonnie and Patricia would take Ryan down to the cottage when Chloe and Rory wanted a break from parenting or if a particular business trip took them out of town. Ryan had an interest in golf and Lonnie got him a second hand set of clubs, mainly to see if he would develop a real interest in the game. Sometimes when on Heckman's Island they would go and play the Lunenburg course; both agreed that you had to be part mountain goat to play it, but it was a golf outing. Lonnie treasured those times with family.

There were other things that needed to be taken care of, such as the sale of the plane, but that did not take much time at all as the other partners quickly bought him out. Any flights in the future would be commercial. Lonnie did not go for his next air medical checkup and so his pilot license expired. He was not concerned; although he enjoyed the freedom of flying it had changed a lot since he first got his license. Gone were the days of flying low along the coast, now you had to set a flight plan which specified your intended elevation and you could not vary that since there were too many other aircraft flying these days and flight path control was very important.

He did get to play more golf, now with Patricia and his kids and his first grandchild. He played about sixty-five percent of his games at the New Ashburn and thirty-five percent at the Old Ashburn. Old Ashburn had just completed a major upgrade to all eighteen greens and the results were excellent. Lonnie hoped they would do some upgrades to the exposed rock areas in some of the fairways soon. Patricia was playing lots of golf with her friends, which worked out well for the both of them. Ashburn would be celebrating its one hundredth anniversary in 2022 and Lonnie had some ideas for the celebrations. He had been a member since 1961 and had several discussions with Gordie Simms, the club manager.

Lonnie and Patricia planned a couple of weeks away in Cape Breton where they had spent their honeymoon. Beverly and Bill joined them for this trip. They played golf at The

Lakes, a new course in Ben Eoin, Bell Bay in Baddeck, Highland Links in Ingonish, Le Portage in Cheticamp, and the new courses on the west coast, Cabot Links and Cabot Cliffs in Inverness. Patricia especially liked Cabot Cliffs because she got her first hole-in-one on the sixteenth hole, a difficult par three to say the least. Patricia was very excited and kept the ball for mounting on a plaque to commemorate the occasion. Plus the fact that Lonnie only had one to date, even with all his years of playing golf. While at the Cabot courses they stayed at the main lodge and enjoyed the ocean views along with the fine dining.

On the agenda for that fall was a cruise on the Danube. The Danube journeys through the very heart of Europe, calling in at some of the world's most elegant, vibrant, and influential cities. The cruise would go through many cities including Budapest, Vienna, Bratislava, and Belgrade. Beverly and Bill had agreed to join them for that trip, so they would have some company from home to share the experience. From the boat they would get to see the history of the European continent pass before them. And of course many of Europe's finest architectural sights are found along this river, something Lonnie was very excited about. Patricia also enjoyed Europe. Perhaps they would spend some of the winter months in Florida or go south of the equator to New Zealand or Australia. Time would tell.

Not quite riding off into the sunset, but retirement sure did have its good points.

About the Author

The author, Donald Lohnes, FRAIC, is a retired architect. He practiced architecture actively for thirty-seven years before retiring in 2008. He was president of the Nova Scotia Association of Architects (NSAA) on two occasions, both during the period of the re-writing of the Nova Scotia Architects Act. In 2007 he was awarded fellowship in the Royal Architectural Institute of Canada (RAIC).

This book takes place mainly in the wonderful province of Nova Scotia. Some of the buildings mentioned were projects undertaken by his firm while others are purely fictional.

During his practice he was involved in a court case, similar to that being described, which is one of the reasons why he wrote this book. Hopefully to raise the awareness for architects and other design professionals that while not committing a crime you can sometimes end up in the courts and that it may not result in a decision that you were expecting.

His first book, titled "So You Want to BUILD a HOUSE," was published in 2014. He resides in Halifax with his wife Pamela.